Symphony of Extinction

By

Njedeh Anthony

This novel is a work of fiction. Any resemblance to actual persons, living or dead, event or occurrence, is entirely coincidental

Dedicated to my niece Isi, now I don't want to get into trouble with my other nieces and nephews, so I have to specify why. She has voraciously read every book I have written and always asks for more. She understands the book characters more than I do. And most importantly, it's absolutely refreshing to learn more about the stories I tell, from her.

Dr. Darshak Khurana

My mother said that I was born under a red moon. When I asked what that meant, she got angry; she said I will never appreciate the magic moment unless I knew why. This even sounded more confusing that her previous statement. Before I was born, my parents emigrated from the city of Gurgaon in India to South Africa because my father, who was a doctor, had a debt that he couldn't pay. He was a gambler and often lost. When he won, he gave never ending sermons on why we should all listen to him. He was charismatic and would be able to talk his way out of hell when he got there. When I was 10, his luck ran out again, causing all of us, namely, my mother and my sister to immigrate to Canada in order to avoid his debt collectors. He had a gift of knowing when to leave places right before death came calling.

I received a full scholarship for a bachelor's degree in biology at the University of Oxford. My mother said that I was blessed; I tried, to no avail, to educate her that I didn't get where I was because I was lucky, but because I was the best.

My theory on my exceptionality was cut short when I met him, Ivan Kozlov. It was hatred at first sight. His full, reddish brown hair was always askew, his clothes were two sizes too small and he didn't notice anyone else in the room. He acted as though nobody had anything else worth saying and the worst part about it was that he didn't acknowledge he was being rude. I knew his type and knew that the only way to bring such a pompous fool back to Earth was to beat him where it mattered: in the grades. For three years in the University of Oxford, I tried to top him in each class, but I was always relegated to second best; the man was a genius and his mind worked like a machine. The worst thing about this Russian was that he didn't bother reading the materials stated in the curriculum, his mind was engaged in other things beyond the scope of study. The other things his mind was on, was a mystery to everyone. It was no secret that I graduated second in our class, but even worse was his carefree attitude at being the best. On our graduation day, I swallowed my pride and asked him for a copy of his thesis. Oddly, he didn't know who I was; he didn't know my name and, to add salt to injury, he gave me his thesis. His thesis, built upon Somatic-cell nuclear transfer and the development of artificial eggs. It could change the world and he handed it to me, including his additional notes and unpublished theories, as though it was toilet paper. The bastard didn't even know my name.

I was 23, 5 feet 8 inches tall with black eyes, a square jaw, and a full head of black hair. On one of the days when my father gambled away the money that I gave to him to help with the bills, I stood and watched him blame his gambling loses on his alcohol consumption. The fact that I earned less than he did and paid for most of the bills wasn't an issue in his argument. I couldn't take it anymore; the man was heading toward rock bottom and was pulling us down with him. We argued, coming close to throwing blows, before he ordered me out of his house. My mother cried and wailed, begging him to change his mind. I didn't understand what my mother was doing with a man like him. However, I gladly accepted his eviction. I told my sister and mother to get their things and follow me. Then, the oddest thing happened. They remained where they were, looking at me in our Arabian-styled living room as though I was an idiot. I never forgave them for that; I walked out of the house and didn't look back. I never looked back.

I completed my Ph.D. at the University of Berkley and, in all that time, not once did I stop being amazed at Ivan's thesis. Without his notes, his thesis was a maze which made Ivan and I the only two people who could decipher the excellence of his work. The thesis was the reason why I specialized in Cellular Biology. Ivan's thesis was about the perfection of the human cell, removing all the preconceived disability in a cell. I spent six years of my life perfecting his thesis. In that time, I figured out how to allow the nuclei in the cell have the capability of enhancement.

Immediately after graduating, I was asked to a meeting at a playground by a red-haired man and his son. They were both over six feet three inches tall and my neck began to hurt as I looked up at them during our conversation. The secrecy of the meeting meant to me that it was significant and that intrigued me. Both the man and his son were named Reagan Knox; the father referred to the son as junior. They were both red-haired, a trait given to them from their Irish background. They were part of a newly–formed, scientific research company called Quad, Inc. This company was completely dependent upon United States military funds. The company had three major shareholders, one of which was the senior Reagan. Due to the sensitivity of the research conducted by the company, the Reagan's chose to be affiliated with it via shell companies. However, with the increase in funding coming into the company, they had decided that they wanted a stronger presence at the company. That's where I came in. I joined Quad, Inc. as a partner. Prior to my joining the company, it had failed in all of its inventions. Somehow, the partners were happy with these failures because everyone was still getting paid, including the Washington politicians who kept fighting for the funds for the company.

My first military contract was to build on the cell enhancement nucleus theory that I had been working on. After 18 months, I came up with a serum that I called the Restart Serum. It enhanced the abilities of the test subjects, making them faster and smarter. The problem was that for the test subjects we tried it on, namely chimps and rats, it worked perfectly for the first three minutes and then the animals died instantly. Suddenly, with the smell of a viable product in the air, everyone wanted the product created yesterday. In no time, I had both the CEO of the company and the military representative, Major Coriolanus Cole, breathing down my neck. The major was black and 42–years-old. He had a few strands of white hair in his thick, black hair.

I was the best there was in the company and I wasn't good enough. I mentioned to them that it was feasible, but, as management works, they only heard that I could make them a product that they could use. At 38, I had a promising career, but with the way this project was going, I was headed toward the blackballed list. I had no choice. I had to find the best. I had to find Ivan Kozlov.

Professor Ivan Kozlov was teaching at Harvard University. My timing at approaching him was impeccable as he had just been passed over for a position to run the Molecular and Cellular Biology Department, a decision that he took as personal. I was given the opportunity to offer him unlimited financial resources to conduct his researches. The best part about it was that the lab was in the Dominican Republic, so he didn't have to deal with the ethical groups or most of the traditional snooping bodies. He said "yes" faster than I expected.

What really confused me was that he probably didn't even remember who I was. All these years, I had him on my mind and he didn't remember me. In the years since we had last seen each other, I had gained a sophisticated look. I was clean shaven and always in a tailored suit. When I was in the lab, I wore a lab coat over it. However, Ivan had remained exactly the same as he had been when we graduated. We both wore glasses; I had tortoise-shell glasses, while he had thick bifocals that looked like goggles. Ivan had a thick beard and bushy eyebrows. Thankfully, he didn't stink.

He read through my notes and, apparently, didn't even notice that most of it was stolen from his notes and thesis. The man had chronic symptoms of ADHD, immediately he became a professor he moved unto other projects. I began to wonder what else this man had created in his basement. In barely a month, he solved my issue and perfected the cell enhancement, allowing the living cells to act in perfect form. The only problem was that the test subjects, after receiving the serum, were unable to sleep. They became restless and ended up killing anything that was placed in their cages.

I was on cloud nine. When I showed the results to the senior Reagan Knox, he became as high as a kite on ecstasy and was quick to show it to Major Coriolanus Cole. We were 90% of the way to the finish line when, suddenly, Ivan's mind diverted to another project. I couldn't reach him; he was in his zone with this new creation. Everyone became angst as we almost had a finished product when he decided to go rogue.

For eight months, I couldn't get him back on topic. He locked himself in the lab and worked on his new project. Even worse was that he used company funds to purchase crates of animal DNA without telling me what he was doing. I wanted to kick him out of the lab, but the scientist in me was too curious about what his mind was creating. Since it took him only a month to solve a problem that I had worked on for 10 years, I was intrigued at what would take him eight months to create.

The management and military were getting impatient and I had to keep stretching my promises. There was only one rule to being on top, you take every credit when you can and, when expecting a big failure, you blame the man below you. I didn't know what Ivan was working on, but I knew that, due to the contracts he signed, that I owned it.

Finally, one day, I heard him screaming in his lab. "We did it! We did it!"

When I walked in, he grabbed me and showed me a Petri dish. Then, he asked me to look through the microscope. I looked and saw a nucleus. I didn't understand what was so important about it and told him that. He asked me to look around the lab. I could see six microscopes on the tables and crates of animal DNA in locked cages all around us. When I said that I still didn't get it, he explained it to me as though I was an ignorant child. He had fused the DNA of 30 animals into a human cell's nuclei. I didn't understand how to accept the abomination, but, then, every major creation in science has been an abomination. Galileo was kept under house arrest by the church for writing that the earth was round. Suddenly, I realized that I was standing in front of history. I could either squash it or embrace it as my own, so I embraced it and we shook hands. I was going to own the project. I asked him to tell me why he picked these particular 30 animals. He said that he picked the bat for echolocation, badger for digging, cheetah for speed, polar bear swimming, fly for the compound eyes, camel for their water storage, lioness for hunting, mice for balance, ants for their strength to carry 10-50 times their weight, jaguar for climbing and dolphins for their adaptability. However, he refused to tell me why he chose the rest of the animals. I did a little snooping and found out that he also used a hedgehog's DNA, but, for the life of me, I couldn't figure out why.

Now that we had agreed to move forward with his experiment, there was only one issue of strong contentious debate: where to get the eggs and sperm needed to create the test tube baby. Ivan wanted to use natural human eggs for the IVF, but the problem was that although our labs were a 100 feet underground in the Mona Island, close to the Dominican Republic, the American press was always snooping around. Therefore, I put my foot down and we used the artificial eggs that we had secretly created in the labs.

The second point of contention was the sperm. Ivan and I were two men of different perspectives. I was polished, he was rugged. I was social, he was anti-social. My legacy came first for me, while science came first for him. The only thing that we had in common was that we were both lonely men with no one to mourn us at our funerals. We had let our passions seclude us from the few people who loved us, namely, our mothers. So, this was our opportunity to bring life into this world and we both wanted it to be ours. Therefore, we decided to try our luck individually.

We fertilized the artificial eggs with 120,000 motile sperms and, in the six days of observations, there was no growth. We kept trying and the fertilization processes never got to the six to eight cell stage. After six months of trying, frustration began to kick in and we began to get desperate. We weren't recording our alterations. Ivan gave up and blamed it all on the artificial eggs, but I had never been so close to history before, so I continued and used all sorts of mindless fertilization processes.

Then, one day, out of the blue, I looked through the microscope and saw that the fertilization process had worked for two tests. The embryos had lived past the eight cell stage. I called the embryos, Adam and Seth. The biggest problem was I wasn't sure how I had gotten it to work as I hadn't taken proper notes.

This ought to have been a thing of joy for Ivan, but, instead, it made him feel like an outsider in the project. He became very pessimistic, openly rooting for the project to fail, hoping that my creation wouldn't continue to grow. He was still adamant that it wasn't feasible for the artificial eggs to work and even accused me of switching the eggs behind his back.

In order to keep suspicion from our lab, Major Coriolanus Cole lured two girls from Sweden, Nova and Astrid, with more money than they could ever imagine. They didn't have any family and he figured that no one would miss them if the experiment went awry. They were 5 feet 8 inches tall, blond with blue eyes; features you would expect to see in a model runway.

Once they arrived at the lab, we conducted the blastocyst transfer. Embryo transfers take three to four growing embryos, a luxury that I didn't have. On average, it takes three IVF cycles to make a pregnancy that takes and I had just one chance. I said "I" because, at this point, Ivan was just an observer; he refused to work on the project anymore.

Nova developed ovarian cancer a month after the IVF and died two weeks after. Astrid, on the other hand, was extremely healthy. At seven months, she was unusually sprite and began to gain strength that was way beyond normal human capacity. She didn't look like she had gained a pound, but she had gained 65 pounds. We began to wonder what was going on. At ten months, she had gained a total of 120 pounds; she began to show, but she wasn't ready to conceive. I began debating whether I should do a C-section and began to speculate as to what the longest gestation period was of the DNA that he added to the nuclei. When I asked Ivan, he suddenly didn't remember what animals he had added. However, when I let him know that Astrid's life depended upon it, he finally told me that he had used black rhinoceros DNA as part of the mix. Their gestation period was 450 days. With this new information, I decided to wait a little longer.

Astrid's room was designed to resemble a five-star hotel; all she had to do was ring the bell by the side of her king-sized bed and a guard would be there to answer to her every whim. She had a Persian rug in her massive bedroom and a large screen TV that received over 300 channels that hung eight feet in the air. Her doors and the walls of her room were made from titanium. We gave her the choice to leave the room whenever she chose, but we also had the ability to lock her in if necessary. She could walk across the underground facility to every office, but she couldn't leave or go to the labs. The facility contained a large kitchen and large auditorium with wall speakers. The entire place was painted white, except Astrid's room, which was azure. There were six other military scientists at the facility and 21 military security guards dressed like civilians so as to not give her the impression that she was in a prison. The only way out of the facility was via an elevator. In order to get the elevator to work, you had to go through a biometric and retina scan.

She was always okay with the way things worked until the first day of the 11th month of her pregnant. On that day, everything changed. She lost her temper because the Swedish channels wouldn't come on in the TV. She acted as though she was having an anxiety attack and then her skin began to open up, revealing a scaly exoskeleton beneath it. She then made an incredible leap to the TV and pulled it out of the wall. Six guards ran into the room to sedate her. As they were trying to calm her down, two died when she flung them across the room like dolls. Two more became permanently disabled; the first when she pounced on him and landed her full weight on his shoulder. The second when she kicked his leg off at the kneecap. The other two guards grabbed their injured colleagues and ran out of the room, locking her inside. I immediately flooded the room with Quinuclidinyl Benziate, which knocked her out immediately. We hurriedly tried to extract the gas from the room as only 0.5 mg was enough to knock out a person and we had flooded the room. As soon as the room was clear, I unlocked it and ran inside to check on her, but she was dead. I had her rushed to the operating room where we conducted a C-section. Cutting into her stomach was much harder than it should have been, but we finally cut through. The soldiers had their weapons pointed at the dead Swedish girl's stomach; nobody was sure what was going to come out. As soon as the stomach was opened, we pulled out the most beautiful boy I'd ever seen. The boy... my son, cried so gently. Everyone else in the room saw a beautiful boy, but I saw a god and called him Adam.

As soon as Adam was born, his mother became nothing, but rotting flesh, which everyone forgot was lying on the table. I shed tears as I carried Adam in my arms. In that moment, my eyes met Ivan's eyes. I hadn't even noticed that he was part of the team who helped me deliver the child. When our eyes locked, we were the only two who existed. I knew what he was thinking, but I didn't care, I had my boy. After the moment, Professor Ivan Kozlov disappeared from existence, nobody, not even the CIA, could find him. Everyone believed him dead because not a dollar was taken from his accounts. It was better for me, the glory was all mine.

The greatest flaw of success is that if you can't replicate it, it becomes a failure. A scientist uses systematic activities to gain knowledge; if the knowledge is achieved and the method to get the knowledge isn't traceable, then the science is missing. Throughout the time that Ivan was working in the lab, I had him on surveillance. I tried to retrace his steps and mine to reproduce Adam's creation, but I failed woefully. There were some missing time feeds on the tapes, but that was normal with the amount of video I had to browse through. Everything that Ivan had told me was either a lie or a half-truth because I was unable to fuse the DNA together properly.

At this time, the company was shamelessly boasting about its achievements to the Hill, which tripled the pressure upon me. I had to feed the wolves, so I gave them the artificial reproductive eggs. That pacified the politicians and my bosses for a while. They were on every network taking credit for the new creation, as though they had created the artificial reproductive eggs. After a few months, they were high on the positive media, which had lasted a few news cycles, and they wanted more. Their expectations continued to grow and the military suddenly wanted to play a bigger part in Quad, Inc. Due to the amount of pressure on me from every angle, I let them know that Ivan did most of the initial work. As such, he became the most searched for man in the world. After months of fruitless results, the general conclusion was that he was dead.

With the inability to recreate Ivan's work, there was only option left, to clone Adam.

Dakota Knox

I am a 26-year-old woman who earned my way to where I am. Given, I'm a 5 feet 7 inches tall, naturally blonde and eye-watering beautiful, white female who works for a defense company, of which my father is a blind subsidiary; however, that doesn't take away the fact that I am a force who should be respected. As soon as I graduated from Harvard Law School, I became a lobbyist for The Quad, Inc. It wasn't my first choice; I wanted to be the vice president of The Knox Holdings, a $560 million portfolio. Instead, I got thrown into the Washington pit of endless corruption. The funny thing is that I am pretty good at this lobbying pyramid or, as some choose to call it, the Washington Game. The scheme is that one legally buys the congressman or senator by donating to his campaign or charity, then you get him to vote for your interest. The funny thing is that the stupid people who vote for them believe anything you want them to believe, as long as you give them the impression that you know what you are talking about.

I have on a tight blue pinstriped suit; the skirt is three inches above my knees, long enough to prevent anyone from thinking of me as a prostitute, but low enough to use my sexuality. Under my suit, I have on a red silk blouse that has a v line showing just the right amount of cleavage. Of course, I have on high heels. I'd feel naked without them. I am sitting in the waiting room at the office of the 55-year-old Senior Senator from Arizona, Senator Holmes. His secretary, a woman about my age, who has a long neck and dresses like a corporate whore, is banging away at the keys of her keyboard. The room is cold and the bastard has left me waiting for 20 minutes after summoning me. It's at times like these when I appreciate congressmen more than senators, they have just two years to do their work. They realize that if they don't play ball, in two years' time, we will replace them. The rug was red and there were pictures of landscapes on the walls.

A buzzer sounded and the secretary picked up the phone without looking at me, even though I was sitting 20 feet from her. She dropped the phone, looked at me with a bland smile and said, "The senator will see you now."

I nodded back, with an appreciative smile; I honestly couldn't stand the long-necked ostrich, but, in DC, you never know when you will need a secretary.

I entered his office holding my brown briefcase; his back was to me as he sat in his swivel chair, staring out the window at the capital. The only things on his desk were a phone and a picture of his family. At the other end of the room was a small, round table surrounded by four chairs. Two high-backed chairs sat opposite his desk. I sat in one, waiting for him to talk.

"I run for office next year, Dakota," he said as he spun the chair toward me. The 5 feet five inches tall senator had gained more weight and seemed unable to button his navy blue suit.

"It will be a landslide; that's if anyone has the guts to run against you," I said and attempted to laugh. The senator's face remained stalwart.

"Did I mention that my daughter's husband works for Vanity Fair?" the senator asked, maintaining eye contact with me, as though I was a prisoner he was interrogating. I attempted to respond, but he kept on talking as though the sound of my voice would dither any form of progress. "Now, he comes to me and asks whether I was aware that The Quad, Inc. has donated to my campaign. And I was like, 'Why are you asking?'" He leans closer on the table, "This is where it gets interesting, he says to me that they might have proof that that company has been cloning." The senator stood and dug his hands into the pockets of his blue trousers, revealing his protruding belly, which was tucked under his white shirt and red tie.

"Cloning!" I exclaimed with a shocked expression.

Abruptly, his hands left his pockets and he banged both of his palms on the table screaming, "Don't you dare lie to me!" The strands of hair that he had left on his head escaped to the front of his face. He took a deep breath and then sat down, talking calmly, "I am going to ask you a few questions and I just want hear the words 'yes' or 'no' come from your mouth."

I said nothing; I just crossed my legs and watched the old fool try to denigrate me.

"Did I rally the congress and Senate to vote for extra funds for The Quad, Inc in the defense bill?"

"Yes," I replied, only after we donated heaven and Earth to get you re-elected, I thought to myself.

"You are aware that Arizona is a republican state?"

"Yes."

"Did you not tell me that the money was used to create some form of serum that would help our soldiers focus more, give them more strength and increase their speed and alertness?"

"The trans-human serum is ready, Senator. We just have to get rid of the insomnia side-effects."

He gave me the disgusted teacher glare and I knew that I had to remember my place in the conversation, so I said, "Yes."

"So," he pulled out a tape-recorder and dropped it onto the middle of the table. "Dakota Knox, I would like you to acknowledge that you are being recorded."

I let the gesture sink in. The fat bastard wanted to have an out at my expense. "I, Dakota Knox, a representative of The Quad, Inc. acknowledge that I am being recorded."

"Did you, in anyway shape or form, mention cloning, either verbally or literally to me, the Whitehouse or any member of congress?"

"No."

"You are aware I am against stem cell research?"

"Yes."

"Does Quad, Inc., or any subsidiary connected with it, engage in cloning?"

"Neither Quad, Inc. nor its subsidiaries engage in human cloning."

As soon as I put 'human' in front of 'cloning,' he raised his eyebrows. Then, he stopped the tape. "Don't you dare screw me on this Knox."

"I wouldn't dare, senator."

He grabbed a few papers from his briefcase and started reading through them, holding a gold fountain pen, as though I wasn't there. I had been around politicians all my life. As a CEO, president or vice president of a company that pays for a politician's campaign, you meet with the politicians after the lobbyist has done the dirty work. Right now, senators and congressmen were like kings, but Citizens United was coming and, when it came, the people with the cash would decide the fate of the senators and congressmen, even the senators would bow to the lobbyist. Unfortunately for me, that time had not yet come.

I picked up my briefcase and said, "Goodnight, senator."

***

I stepped off the 747 jet at 1:42 in the morning. Waiting in the company's limousine was Major Coriolanus Cole, an imposing black man. As soon as I got into the car, the driver stepped out of the car, leaving us alone with the engine running on the airport runway. I sank into the leather seat opposite the major. He was a true soldier in every word; he followed orders and never asked questions. His superiors made him the face representing the project because they knew he would take the fall if necessary and not take anyone down with him. He was six feet two inches tall and his body was hard, as though carved with stone.

"Its 1:43 in the morning," he said in a deep voice. He was attempting to be sarcastic, but his stiff nature made the words sound serious.

"Tell me something I don't know," I said as I looked around the limo. I had made sure my assistant was swept the car for bugs, yet I was still a little paranoid. "Someone sang."

"How much do they know?"

"Just the cloning…" I sighed, to make him appreciate my decision. "Purge the Adam project," I ordered.

"How deep a purge are we talking?" he asked.

"Everything not connected with the serum... except Adam."

"I'll have to pass that request through the general," he said, emotionless.

"I don't give a damn who you have to pass it through. Everything needs to be purged. Somebody in our little circle talked." I pointed my two index fingers at each other and said, "We are all this close to going to jail. And when I mean all, I mean all, your general, my father, every one of us."

"And Dr. Khurana?" he asked.

I opened the door, stepped out and looked back at him. "He lives... for now."

Major Coriolanus Cole

A soldier is never born a soldier; he is made into one. He realizes that his number one family isn't the woman who could divorce him for any reason nor is it the spoiled children who will grow up and forget his number, instead, it is the men who fight beside him and would die to protect him. I have no respect for any man who doesn't serve his country. My two sons, Kyle and Eli, are 14 and 12. When they are of age, it's not open for debate, they are signing up for service. When you look into the eyes of a soldier who has seen battle, man or woman, you will never understand what lies behind those eyes unless you've been there yourself. Call me sexist, but any woman who is a soldier, who has seen battle, is not a woman to me, but a soldier. I have said it a thousand times, there is nothing as precise as a female sniper.

General Timothy Murray asked me to pick the finest soldiers I knew for a clandestine mission. I served under the man in the U.S. invasion of Panama; he was a commanding officer I was proud to serve under. I did as he asked and picked 25 of America's bravest warriors. Now, I am standing in the general's study about to negotiate for their lives. The general's study had barely 50 books on the shelves, there was a glass cabinet with a set of six crystal glasses, three bottles of bourbon, a bottle of scotch and a whiskey bottle in it. A brown sectional sofa and love seat sat against a cream-colored wall. A coffee table sat next to the love seat. I stood fully dressed in my regalia, standing at attention, waiting for my general. The room was cold, about 45 degrees. The floors were wooden and the window gave a view of the manicured lawn. An office table and chair sat beside the window. The general walked into the room in his pajamas and house coat, a glass of bourbon in his hand.

"Its 5:30 in the morning, Coriolanus. You woke up the Mrs.," he said as he stood right in front of my face. General Murray was bald and white. He was the same height as me, but his face was round, while mine was oblong. He was also 20 pounds heavier, which showed in all the wrong places.

"I am sorry, sir, but I talked with the Knox woman. We need to purge ourselves from the situation," I said.

He walked to his cabinet, took out a bottle of bourbon and filled his glass. "Civilians are ungrateful vultures. They are quick to shout human rights, but demand security for their children. They don't want to get their hands dirty to secure the country; they just want to enjoy their clean lives, while we have blood on our hands. If we left this country to the liberals, terrorists would have the right to change our amendments." The general sighed, sat down on the sofa and set the glass on the coffee table. "My hands are tied."

"My men are loyal, sir. They don't talk."

"Somebody did," he said as he rubbed his hand on his forehead. "I know your men. They all have exemplary backgrounds, but we are dealing with Washington. They fear scandals more than bullets. We need to tie up every loose end."

"You asked for my best men, sir."

"Nobody is asking you to pull the trigger."

I bit my lip, not losing eye contact, "They are fathers, mothers, sons, daughters, grandfathers, patriots-"

"They are soldiers!" the general yelled as he gulped down his bourbon. "They are dying for their country. Their families will be taken care of, far more than the VA could."

"I...would request to see the same fate as my men."

"You request to see the fate as your man," the general said and then scoffed. "Do you think you belong to you?" He stood up and walked over to me, standing inches from my face, "Tracing down my descendants, there has never been a male member of my family who wasn't an altar boy. I went to my priest during confession. This is a man who heard all of the atrocities I did in Vietnam and told me that my sins were forgiven. When I told him there were 15 identical one-year-old human beings in an underground structure in the Dominican Republic, he spat on my face and told me never to come again for confession."

My expression gave way to my sudden euphoria, "The priest must have told someone about the clones."

The general sighed and walked away from me to stand in front of the window. "I wish. As soon as I stepped out of the booth, I bugged him. He hasn't told a soul. He hasn't even confessed it yet." My demeanor went back to somber as he asked, "Why do we do the things we do?" He clasp his hands behind his back and, not waiting for my response, continued. "Our enemies aren't following the rules of morality. In order to survive, we have to be ahead of the curb. We have to be ahead of innovation. Whoever controls technology, controls the future," he said. He walked back over to me and put his hands on my shoulders. "Your soldiers are not dying for nothing…" I could feel his hot breath on my face, "they are dying for their country." There was a deep frown on my face when he said, "Lieutenant Colonel."

"You are promoting me for killing my men?" I asked in disgust.

"I am promoting you for doing your job! You are dismissed," he said as he walked back to the window, turning his back to me as I plodded out of the room.

**

There is something about 3 am that wakes up the demons in the world around us. I drove the Jeep toward the mountain on Mona Island on the narrow, twisty and spiraling road until I got to the bungalow. I could see the tower antenna of the underground facility, which was still three miles away. On the surface, we gave the impression that we were constructing a radio broadcasting station, but underneath it was were all of the magic was done.

Dr. Khurana walked out of his house, sleepy-eyed, wearing only white boxer shorts and a white shirt. The lights from the Jeep shined brightly into his eyes and he shielded them from the light. If I was anyone else, he would have had a fit, but he was scared of me and that worked to my advantage.

"Is there a problem?" he asked, walking toward me.

"Where is Adam?"

"Which one? There are 15 of them," he said sarcastically.

"The original."

"He is with me." Then, he continued defensively, "When we put the original Adam with the clones, the toddlers banded together and attacked him. If they were a year older, they might have succeeded. With their abilities, I thought it will be-"

"Bring him out here and put on some damn pants," I said, disgusted. The man ran into the house, following my orders. I took out the radio transmitter from the glove compartment and spoke in it, "The falcon will be out of the nest in five."

Dr. Khurana came out of the bungalow holding the blond, blue-eyed, sleeping two-year-old in his arms, like a parent. The man was attached to the child, an observation that I decided I needed to report to my superiors. He got into the backseat with the child. I got in at the same time and, as soon as they were secure, I drove off. He was silent as we drove down the road. He didn't ask where we were going. Either his fear had overridden his curiosity or he knew where we were going.

"Tell me about India, Dr. Khurana?"

"I can't. I've never been there," he replied, fear lacing his words.

"I have never been to Africa. I should rephrase that, I have never been to West Africa. I've been deployed to Northern Africa." I looked at him through the rearview mirror and found that he was as nervous as hell, just how I wanted him to be.

"Are you going to kill me?" he asked. I almost felt sorry for the pompous bastard. I ignored him and continued driving. "Please, whatever you do to me, don't kill the boy. He's just a child. He knows nothing. Nobody has to know that he lives."

I looked at the child in the rearview mirror. For some ungodly reason, he reminded me a little of

Reagan Knox. For the first time, I also noticed the similarities between him and the doctor.

The doctor suddenly looked up, following the white trail of smoke that quietly sailed through the sky until it landed on the facility. The explosion that followed made the ground around us shake. I drove faster down the hill.

"You, Adam and I are the only ones they want alive," I said stiffly, as tears began streaming down my face. I mourned my soldiers, my brothers…my family. "Someone in that facility leaked a story about the clones to the media. So, now, there are only seven people alive who know about the Adam project." I thought of the names in my head: General Murray, Dr. Khurana, Reagan Knox, Sr., Reagan Knox, Jr., Dakota Knox, the priest and myself. I forgot one more person, one person who had the entire project circling in his hand: Adam. I looked in the rearview mirror at the sleeping Adam; the last and most important piece of our little circle.

Professor Matthew Ryan

I left Russia because there were over a hundred people like me. I left England after graduating from Oxford because of the systematic caste system they proudly lived under. I left Harvard because the internal politics within the system would put congress to shame. I left Quad, Inc. because I was cheated out of my destiny.

Months prior to my exit from Quad, Inc., I knew it was time to leave. Dr Darshak… I keep forgetting his last name…anyway, he insisted on using artificial eggs, instead of real eggs from a woman's ovary. At that point, I realized that I was not in control of my project. That was one insult I couldn't take. Given, the artificial egg was an impressive creation on his part, but that was the height of this man's scientific accolades. After he rebuffed my suggestion to use real human eggs, I slowly began taking samples home and working from my place. I figured out the issues with the failed tests, which happened when the chromosomes were being created by merging the fused DNA to the human DNA strands. So, I perfected the fused DNA and made a few alterations to the mitochondria and lysosomes. I thought about sharing the technology with Darshak, but, at the time, he had already succeeded in getting the Swedish girls pregnant. Although, I still think foul play was involved with Darshak using the artificial eggs.

Regardless, I decided it was time to move on. So, I moved my samples to a preservation facility in Spain.

I didn't have to be Einstein to understand the sensitivity of what we did. I knew there was no way they would let me quit and disappear from the island alive. I knew too much, so I bid my time and secured a fake passport with a new identity. If I left on an ordinary day, in less than 24 hours they would notice my absence. So, I waited and waited. On the day that Adam was born, I saw my opening and I was gone. That was the day that Professor Ivan Kozlov died and Professor Matthew Ryan began to exist. Something about education, you sacrifice years of your life for that prestige, it's almost impossible to forget, so I chose to remain a biologist. I didn't change my educational background, but I toned down my achievements down to the minimum.

I began to teach undergraduate courses at Al Manar University in Tripoli. In six months, I was not anywhere finding any female subject to fuse the DNA; the country was too conservative for my experiment. I needed a country a little looser with its morality. I needed a country that didn't see its citizens as its most prized possessions. So I applied for jobs in mostly corrupt countries. The University of Port-Harcourt in Nigeria offered me a job. The university offered to take care of all of my expenses and, even though the pay was much less than what I was currently making, for what I wanted to do it worked, so I moved.

For the first three months, I taught graduate biology and chemistry courses at the university. The country was very humid; whenever I stepped out my door, I was drenched in sweat. The corruption in the country was beyond my expectations. The police literally stood in the streets taking money from transportation vehicles in which the people didn't have the right registrations. The transportation vehicles were like pieces of junk metal joined together and they were always packed to over capacity. At the university, electricity was constant because it came from generators. Outside the university, the Nigerian Electric Power Authority controlled the electricity and when they provided four to five hours of electricity a week, they expected the citizens to be grateful. The roads had potholes everywhere. The senators earned more than the American president, yet they did literally nothing. The only thing I loved about the country was the people. The people were so happy; those who lived in poverty always found a reason to be happy. When they saw a foreigner, white, Asian, Hispanic, Arab, it didn't matter, they treated them like guests, eager to help. I hadn't met a Nigerian yet who had xenophobic traits.

The three bedroom bungalow in which I stayed was at the furthermost end of the college campus. The entrance door led directly to the kitchen. Beside the door was a moderately small living room. The three bedrooms were spread out in the three corners of the building. There was one bathroom in the house. The living room contained cane chairs and tables. A fluorescent light hung from the ceiling next to a ceiling fan that was always oscillating, making a creaking sound. There were lots of trees on the borders of the campus, especially right next to where I lived. The house was isolated and the other members of the faculty were pretty good about giving each other their privacy. However, like the culture of the country, when they did visit, they deemed it unnecessary to announce it. It was one of those situations where they felt it rude for a member of the same community to be a stranger. The city of Port-Harcourt cared about only one thing, living life to the fullest. I have to admit that I fell in love with the city. Ironically, for the first time in my life, this reddish brown haired, 40-year–old, white man felt at home in an ocean of blackness.

By the second month, my honeymoon was over. I had to do what I had come here to do. In a town called Choba, the road that lead to the highway had a fork in it, one fork led to a river and the other led to the university. At that junction, there was a wooden house, which was rare in this country as most of the houses were made of bricks. Due to overcrowding and the burning sun, most people hopped on bike cabs called okada to get from place to place. One day, I got on an okada and went to this wooden house. Music from the artist Fela boomed from speakers in the house. Inside the house was a bar. Men were seated on wooden benches, their drinks lined the table. The room was dark, except for a dim, red bulb. Next to the bar was a hallway. On the other side of the hallway, outside 10 x 10 wooden booths, were the ladies of the night. Four of the booths were occupied. When I walked in, five available women rushed me as though I was leaking dollar bills. They pulled me in all directions. Only one stayed seated. She was sitting in a chair, wearing a red miniskirt and torn tank top. Her name was Nkiru. She was 23-years-old, 5 feet 7 inches tall and skinny. Her hair was braided backward. Her bosoms weren't well endowed like her comrades, but she had a beautiful face. Once the other women saw that I had my eye on her, they let go of me. We negotiated for the night and she came home with me.

Once she was in the bungalow, she began to take off her clothes. However, I stopped her. "I don't want to do any of that."

Nkiru looked at me suspiciously and took a few steps away from me. "So, what do you want us to do?" Like most Nigerians, the English language and Broken-English were the only languages in common in a country with over 500 languages. It was expected of a majority of Nigerians to speak both, especially if they lived in a university town.

"This is going to be an awkward request," I said as I pulled a cane chair out for her and sat down in a chair opposite her. "I will like you to…" I scratched my head, still figuring out how to say the words.

She kept looking around, still suspicious of the environment; she was apparently new to the profession and kept pulling her little brown purse to her chest.

"I will like you to have a child for me and basically remain here for the nine months you are pregnant."

She looked at me and, for the first time, there wasn't fear in her eyes, there was just pity. She stood up, gently counted the 600 naira I gave her to spend the night and said, "I am sorry." She handed the money to me.

I was never good with women; honestly, I couldn't remember talking this long with a woman without it involving science. "I will pay you far more than you expect."

"Take your money!" she ordered me, her voice still sounded soothing even though she was trying to be forceful.

"You keep it," I said. I went to the door and opened it, "I am sorry for wasting your time."

She stopped by the door, looked and me and asked, "How much?"

"$25,000." She smiled; she didn't believe me. "If you do this, you will get $5,000 upon insemination." She arched her eyebrows and I realized that I needed to tone down the language. "To start with, I will give you a thousand if you agree to this, then $5,000 when you get pregnant, $4,000 after your first trimester or… after three months of pregnancy, then another $5,000 after six months and when you give birth I will give you 10 thousand."

"Dollars?" she asked, arching her eyebrows.

"Dollars, not naira."

"And I will stay here."

"Yes, you can go to the market, around campus, but no trips. Nobody except the people at the university will see us together as a couple."

"You want to marry me?" she asked confused.

"No!" I said quickly. "No, no, no. I just want to get you pregnant."

She looked again at the rooms. It was no secret what she was thinking, "Now."

"I'm sorry, I should have made myself clear," I said. I still had a slight Russian accent, but the American way of talking was more evident. "It will be by artificial insemination… I won't be having intercourse with you when I get you pregnant."

She stood, confused, for a moment; her demeanor was angelic, yet she didn't give away anything from her expression. "Okay," she said.

The plan was to keep the rest of the information to myself, but there was something about her innocence that pulled the truth out of me. "The embryos are not fully human and there is a very strong possibility that..." I bit my lips before I continued, "that you might die."

She looked me dead in the eye after I said those words. I knew she only had a primary school education, but anyone over the age of four understood the word die. She said nothing. She just walked out of my house and I was all alone again in my empty bungalow.

Three weeks later, I came home after an evening class and saw her on my doorstep. She held a large plastic bag, which they called a Ghana-must-go. It was sparsely filled with clothes. She stood up as I approached her as though I was some form of royalty and she couldn't sit before me.

"Is there a chance I will live?" she asked.

"I will try."

"I will need $1,230 to pay to get back our land, $720 for mother's eye surgery, $620 for my oldest brother's dowry, $520 for my youngest brother's tomato business, $450 for my sister's annual rent at the university and $2,000 for my husband's sand business. Can I get this amount first or is it too much?"

As soon as she said this, I felt a chill run through my veins. She was prostituting herself for her family, including a shameless husband. Then, reality hit me, the country's previous president, Ibrahim Babangida, had given his seal of approval to anyone who scammed foreigners. Corruption was on the rise, the poor were getting poorer and the rich were getting richer. People were getting desperate; people were scamming their own family members. It got so rampant that they gave it a name, 419. Looking at this girl, whom I believed was telling me the truth, I realized that I couldn't get myself to give her the money.

"I will give you the money immediately after insemination, but not before."

She sighed and remained standing, looking at me. I didn't understand why, but it took me a moment to figure out that she was waiting on me to open the door, which I quickly did. I helped with her bag and showed her to her room. I used the third room as my private lab. At that point, I realized one tiny thing, Matthew Ryan didn't have $25,000 dollars, Ivan Kozlov did.

It had been over 18 months since I left the lab. I was hopeful that the hounds weren't still trailing my scent. If they did, this was definitely going to give me away. I did a wire transfer of my funds and bounced it around 28 accounts all over the world until I picked it up in Switzerland and then disappeared again. I still had $187,000 left, after I withdraw $87,000 dollars. I didn't want to take most of it because I felt it would really draw attention. I used the money to get my home lab into a perfect state. Then, I made my initial payments to Nkiru and the experiment began.

Nkiru was very comfortable staying in the house; maybe it was the constant electricity or just the peacefulness of where we were located. I had a houseboy who used to stay with me, do the cleaning and cooking, but, with the nature of what we were going to engage in, the utmost secrecy was required, so I let him go. Nkiru, on her own prerogative, took it on herself to do the cleaning, cooking and, basically, make the house a home. She began growing vegetables outside the house. She made me feel like a king, although we didn't have much to talk about. However, the idea of coming home to someone who took care of me was oddly fulfilling.

I had 12 growing embryos. I used four in the first IVF cycle and they worked like a charm. She became pregnant faster than I expected. During the first trimester, I noticed nothing different about Nkiru. She gained only 20 pounds. During the second trimester, she gained 60 pounds. She looked like a different woman; her weight was evenly spread out over her body. She suddenly became exceptionally sprite and, then, the weirdest thing began to happen, her hunger for knowledge began. She read everything in the house: the chemistry books, the biology books, anything she could get her hands on, even the dictionary. I kept bringing books home from the library for her to read. Her craving for food, at this time, was also out of this world. She had the appetite of six heavyweight wrestlers. I began to fear at this point, because I remembered the Swedish girl followed the same path, except that instead of reading, the Swedish girl was always watching the television. I began to think about what I could do differently with Nkiru to get a different end result. All of my neighbors thought Nkiru was my wife. They believed that I paid her dowry and did the traditional African wedding. Both she and I were happy with their assumptions; it prevented her from being chastised and them from suspecting anything abnormal.

The geology professor, who lived next to me, had two dogs, a poodle and bulldog. The poodle was allowed to roam the house, but the bulldog was caged and barked like a demon at anyone and anything it sensed walking past the front of his territory. That led to my epiphany. The Swedish girl, Astrid, was allowed to walk around the facility, but, with her growth of intelligence, she knew she was a prisoner. If you cage an animal, it will become violent, but if you let it free, it becomes a much gentler creature.

Nkiru and I, at this time, had the best conversations. We talked about science and she began to teach me about literature and art. One evening, we sat on the cane chairs outside the house looking at the full moon.

"How are you feeling?" I asked.

"Fine," she replied, smiling.

"I think you should visit your family," I said.

She let the words digest and the wheels in her head began turning. Then, she said, "You want me to leave?"

"No, no, no, not at all."

"Then why?"

"I don't want you to feel..." I didn't know how to tell her that I was trying to avoid her feeling like she was my prisoner. I wanted to tell her that I needed her much more than the unborn child. I wanted to tell her that I was having the best days of my life. I wanted to tell her that I... I... loved her.

"I am happy. Do not worry about how I feel," she said as she stood. Her hands gently caressed my shoulder as she walked back into the house.

She had to live. I needed her alive. I began debating doing a C-section to get whatever she had inside of her out, but I wasn't a medical surgeon and I knew the risk outweighed the reward. So, I waited, prayed and observed, hoping that what happened to Astrid would not happen to her.

During the 10th month, Nkiru had gained 180 pounds, more than Astrid had. I began to dread that she would suffer the same fate as Astrid and I didn't know what to do. I took a leave of absence from the university to watch her. As I slept in the middle of a Sunday night, I woke up when my queen size bed broke. I found Nkiru on the floor. She had come into my room and sprightly sat on the bed, and her weight had broken it. In her room, she had a mattress on the floor because her bed had broken earlier in the week.

"Are you okay," I asked as I rushed to help her get up.

She chose to remain on the floor. Then, she crawled to the center of the broken bed and said ever so   gently, "The baby is coming."

"The baby is coming? The baby is coming!" I yelled. I got up and started to leave the room.

She grabbed me. "Where are you going?"

"I need to get my keys to take you the hospital," I said frantically.

"We don't know what is inside me."

"You have a child inside you."

She smiled. Then, she raised her sleeping gown to reveal her belly. I turned around.

"You're going to deliver the child, so this is not the time to play the gentleman."

I turned to her and she said, "This is no child." She tapped her belly three times and moving contours developed on her belly. Then, I saw a baby's handprint and a hand tapped back three times from inside the womb. I stood in awe, my mouth hanging open.

"It's time to get it out of me," she said.

"How do you know it's time?"

"My water broke," she said matter-of-factly. "Get hot water and towels and lots of towels."

"Okay, okay, okay," I said frantically, confused as to where to go.

"Relax and breathe," she said. Her legs were already spread apart, ready to give birth.

"Don't you feel any pain?" I asked confused as to why I was the only one tense.

"I feel no pain," she said with a straight face.

I ran to the kitchen, got a ring boiler and placed it in a green bucket to get the water hot. I ran to the bathroom and gathered three towels. Then, I ran back to the bucket, but the water had already heated some. I took out the ring boiler and began carrying the green bucket and three towels to the bedroom. I took two steps away from the kitchen and then walked back and got a stainless steel basin. I walked back to the bedroom. When I entered the room, my heart broke at what I saw.

Nkiru's back was against the wall. She looked radiant and, in front of her, was a baby. She had her mother's eyes and complexion. The baby didn't show any trace of me in her. The baby's eyes were open; the sheets were wet, with just a few patches on blood her forehead. She cried as she stretched her tiny little fingers toward Nkiru; she knew her and knew that she was her mother. Nkiru, on the other hand, had disassociated any maternal connection to the baby; she moved further away from the child, the umbilical cord was the only thing tying them together. I quickly went to the child and picked her up, holding her in my arms. As soon as she was in my embrace, she looked at me, stopped crying, smiled and slept.

"Cut it off me!" Nkiru screamed. The baby opened her eyes and then closed them again.

I stretched my hand to the dresser next to the bed and got out some scissors and pegs. I cut off the umbilical cord and pegged it. As soon as I cut it, Nkiru ran out of the room like a bat out of hell to the shower. I walked out of my room with the baby. I had converted the lab into a baby's room with baby monitors and sensor cameras. I gently placed her in the crib as she slept.

I walked into the hallway and heard the shower running. I waited outside the door and asked, "Are you okay?" After 15 minutes, I asked again, "Nkiru, are you okay?" There was still no answer. I opened the door and saw Nkiru sitting in the shower, crying, still in her gown.

"Nkiru, are you okay?" I asked her, scared if she was going through a mental breakdown.

"It's not human," she said. "It came out of me."

"You are in shock," I said. I turned off the shower and picked her up, her shoulder resting on mine. Both her legs were under my elbow, her soaked body drenching me. I took her to her room, undressed her, dried her with a towel and put a set of fresh clothes on her. I placed her on her mattress on the floor, the same way that I had placed the child in her crib. Her room had brown curtains and a wide oak wardrobe filled with the clothes that she had gotten in the last months. She had a lamp on her wooden dresser. On her walls and in the living room, were many pictures of us.

Just as I was about to leave, she looked at me and said, "Stay with me, just for tonight."

It was clear what she wanted. She was asking me to choose between her fragile state and a baby who was less than half an hour old. I chose her; I held her in my arms, waiting for her to sleep, so I could check on the baby.

I don't know when or how it happened, but I fell asleep. I wasn't a deep sleeper, but I just got lost in my dreams. I opened my eyes and Nkiru wasn't in bed with me. I presumed she was making breakfast, but when my eyes fell on the wall, I saw that all of the pictures were gone. Then, I noticed that her wardrobe was half empty. I quickly jumped to my feet and ran out the room. I checked everywhere before I saw a note on a cane chair. I couldn't bring myself to read it; I knew that she was gone. I sat alone on the cane chair and a sudden flood of loneliness overwhelmed me. I couldn't breathe. I hated myself for letting anyone into my life. It was then that I heard the most beautiful sound in my life. I heard my daughter cry. I walked into the room and there she was, crying. This time, my embrace wasn't enough, so I gave her the ready-to-go baby formula that I had in her room and fed her. While she fed, she occasionally stopped, looked at me and laughed, then continued eating. Eve was a carbon copy of her mother. Eve… yes, Eve, that was her name.

Dr. Darshak Khurana

When Adam was 5-years-old, he was 4 feet 5 inches and had golden hair and catlike eyes. He didn't say much, but, when he did, his words swallowed the room. He was always angry, a trait he might have gotten from me; I had never seen him smile. We lived in an isolated historic brick farmhouse in the middle of the woods in Easton, Maryland. The house was totally renovated inside and out. There were four bedrooms and two bathrooms in the two story building. It had wooden floors and two garages. Our next neighbor lived five miles away and deer often roamed passed the house until the day Adam could walk. Then, they never returned.

On the porch was a wooden swing. Adam sat on it, wearing rainbow shorts, a grey tee-shirt and a blue hooded sweatshirt "He is coming," he said.

It was no secret who "He" was. We had only had one visitor who wasn't either a Jehovah's Witness or Mormon: Colonel Coriolanus Cole. I walked out onto the porch and saw Adam looking straight ahead of the house into the woods. There was no one there. I couldn't hear anything. There was about a mile of road, made of sand and broken branches, between our house and the main road. I waited on the porch because Adam was never wrong. After five minutes, I heard the Colonel driving toward us in his black Range Rover. He stopped in front of the house and I walked down the three steps from the porch to the driveway to meet him. The Colonel was dressed in his blue uniform.

"Dr, Khurana," he said.

"Colonel Cole, Congratulations on your promotion," I said. He ignored me. "We've known each other for a while, Colonel, you can call me Darshak."

"Dr. Khurana," he said, his face stiff and his eyes focused on Adam. "We know who sent the leaks to the reporter," he said as his haunting dark gaze fell upon me. He was an intimidating man; there were patches of white hair around his full black hair.

I kept eye contact with him as I responded, "Who was it?"

"Kozlov," he replied, walking past me and sitting next to Adam.

"He is alive?" I asked, genuinely shocked.

"How are you?" the colonel asked Adam.

Adam ignored him and I quickly responded. "He is tired and a little cranky."

The colonel looked at me and he knew I was lying for Adam. "We should talk in private," he said, walking past me into the woods. I followed him as he continued to move deep into the woods.

When I was sure that we were as far enough away from the house to not be heard, I asked, "Did you read my notes?"

"Yes, I read your notes and, honestly, I am tired of reading notes," He towered over me and said, "We need him in training."

"He is a five-year-old boy," I said, incredulously, resting my back against an oak tree.

The colonel looked around at the red oak trees, which towered over 60 feet, and then said, "You remember that he is a property of the United States?"

"Yes, I do, but we, we, we, need to not forget-"

"You are wasting my time."

"Listen!" I said, agitated. "If you push him the wrong way, instead of having the greatest war machine for the army, you will have the most dangerous one against it." He didn't say anything, but kept eye contact. "You put him in a cage and he will destroy us all," I said. Then, I took a step away from the tree.

"You realize that the Adam project has cost us over 95 million dollars?"

"I wasn't aware of that."

"Now, you are," he said as he marched toward his car. Then, he asked, "How long do you want to keep handling him with kid gloves?"

"Five more years."

He stopped with his back to me. The silence of the woods was deafening, "You're joking," the colonel said.

"We don't fully understand him. Whenever he is uncomfortable with the environment, he enters a cocoon state like he did last year. If we push him back to his cocoon state, nobody knows how long he will remain in the cocoon state this time."

The colonel sighed, "There is a new scientist of whom everyone is singing his praise, Doctor Lin. He created a way to get a missile to track a human being within 500 feet based on his DNA and kill him." He let his words sink in. I was being replaced. He walked back through the woods to his Range Rover and angrily drove off.

I stood between the towering trees, massaging my head. I had witnessed this man wipe out his own men because he was ordered to; the way things were, he might convince his superiors to kill me. I felt the ground shake as Adam jumped to the ground from the top of the 60 foot tree.

I had seen Adam jump off a hill, a webbed skin grew out from between his hips to his elbows and he glided in the air like a bird; so, watching him jump down from a tree was not an exciting event.

"You leaked the story to the reporters about the clones," Adam said, his words sharp.

"Why did you say that?"

"You heart rate increased when he mentioned the leaks," he said as he stood in front of me, almost as if he was interrogating me.

"Yes, I did."

"Why?"

"They were abominations," I said. "No one has the right to clone a god."

Adam smiled and started to walk back toward the house. He stopped after twenty paces, "As long as I live, I will be the only one to kill you, no one else. Do you understand me?"

"Yes," I said. Then, he walked back toward the house, with the god-like audacity that he possessed.

Dakota Knox

Senator John Holmes made a stroke with his golf club; my father, my brother and I quickly gave a resounding applause as we watched the ball move toward its goal. In all honesty, it was an appalling shot, but Senator Holmes was the chairman of the Defense Committee, so we weren't the only ones who had to kiss his butt. The man had bypass surgery done and had lost weight, but his skinnier look made him look older. Reagan Knox Jr., my brother, was acting as his caddy.

The man looked at us, "That was a lousy stroke and you knew it," he said.

"I couldn't have made a better shot," my brother said as he smoothly brown-nosed his way into the conversation.

"Reagan," the senator turned to my father. "Kids will say what they have to say to get a better report card. So, I am going to ask you to tell me straight. The restart serum or the enhanced serum, whatever it is called, does it exist?"

"If it doesn't exist, then it means that I scammed the United States army," my father said, attempting to smile. The senator stared at him blankly. My father put his hands in his hair, which was turning from red to white, "Colonel Cole follows every step of our progress; the serum exist. We-"

"Six months, Reagan. I want an exhibition in six months. You can call it classified or whatever you want," the senator said, as he walked away.

"Don't you dare walk away from me?" my father commanded. The senator looked back at him, shocked. "I take your crap and I digest it because I am making money from it, but don't, for one second, think that you are doing me a favor. I put you where you are and I can take you out. Maybe you've forgotten but there will soon be unlimited contributions we can make through groups for the candidates of our choice."

"Six months, Reagan," he repeated. Then, he got in his golf cart. My brother rushed after him with the golf clubs and they drove away.

"What do we do now?" I asked.

"What I want from you are grandchildren!" he yelled.

I looked at him a little puzzled, trying to figure out what that had to do with what I had asked.

He looked around the course, as though getting his bearing on the conversation, then he said, "We have two choices: show off Adam or do the experiments."

"The colonel said we needed five more years before the boy is ready."

Father took a handkerchief from the pocket of his brown trousers, which he used to wipe sweat of his forehead. "Five more years!? Do they think this is all a joke?"

"I could talk to Khurana myself."

"No!" Father exclaimed. "I want you as far from this debacle as possible." He used his left hand to massage his neck. "We need to do the experiment."

"What about the side effect?"

"Dr. Khurana has had over five years to correct the issue. In six months, we have no choice, we need human tests," he said as he walked over to our golf cart. I followed behind. "This time, Dr. Lin needs to be the lead on everything."

"What happens after the experiment?"

He sighed and looked at me as I got into the driver's seat. "Money isn't power. It's a step lower than fame. Power is power and that bastard has it. You will be running for congress, then the Senate. We need to bring the power into the family."

I looked at him confused.

"Drive," he commanded and I drove off.

Colonel Coriolanus Cole

People join the army for their country, family tradition, the paycheck or to legally kill others. It was unfortunate that, in my quest for human subjects for the trans-human serum, I only had the two worst candidates left from the screening process: the patriot and psycho, both private first class soldiers in the army. The first man was ready to die for his love of country, while the other man was hoping to die like a video game character. There were no other soldiers ready to sacrifice their life for the experiment. Their names were Hosie and Bubba. Both were 5 feet 8 inches tall. Hosie was 20-years-old, while Bubba was 21-years–old. Hosie was a black–haired, well-built Hispanic man, who came to the United States with his parents as illegal immigrants, originally from El Salvador. Bubba was white, had red hair and was five pounds overweight with tanned red skin. He was originally from an isolated town in Mississippi. Bubba joined the army because his girlfriend got pregnant and he didn't want to deal with a pregnant girlfriend or a screaming child and he felt that it was a perfect opportunity to kill a man and get paid for doing it. The army had dropped their standards when the wars in Afghanistan and Iraq began, so they were willing to recruit Bubba even after he failed his drug tests. Unfortunately for both men, in the field they… let me look for the best way to put this… they were physical disgraces to the uniform. In no time, they were designated to pouring coffee, shining shoes, cutting potatoes and typing letters.

I walked into the room and both men stood at attention. "At ease," I said.

Both men stood at ease with their hands behind their backs. We stood in a white walled room that didn't have any windows. There were only three chairs in the room. A camera sat in front of them.

"For the interest of legal action, I would like you to acknowledge that everything you say or do is being recorded in this room." The men remained stiff, looking at me, "Acknowledge."

"I acknowledge that I am being recorded," both men said in unison, Bubba's voice was higher than Hosie.

"Gentleman," I said as I stood over them, "you are aware that this trans-human serum has never been tried on a human." They nodded their heads. "From the experiments done on rats, which have similar body systems to ours, the side effect has led to lack of sleep, which caused homicidal tendency in the rats. If chosen, we intend to put you in a sleeping chamber where you will spend at least 40 hours each week. The manner in which you want the 40 hours sleeping time assigned to you is your prerogative, to remedy this side effect. Beyond that, we are not aware of any other side effects, but I almost guarantee you that more exist. We just don't know about them yet as the rats were not able to communicate them with us." I watched the two young men for a moment and it just didn't feel right. I stood in front of Bubba and stared at him. "When you take this serum, you will be faster and smarter. Your focus will be pristine. How can the army guarantee your loyalty?"

A dark smile threatened the side of Bubba's chaffed lips, "I have no idea, sir."

I walked over to Hosie, "With this serum, you can jump over 15 feet. You will have five times the stamina of a marathon runner. Your strength will be more than any living man. You will always have the drive of a man on steroids. Why should the army entrust that kind of power to you?"

"Because I am ready and willing to die as a guinea pig for the uniform."

I arched my eyebrows. I didn't expect that answer and there was no trace of sarcasm in his tone. I sat down in the chair across from them and rubbed my nose. "When you leave this room, there will be two doors in front of you. The door to the left leads you to the outside. The door to the right leads you to a lawyer who will require you to sign some disclaimers... My son is close to your ages; I wouldn't want him doing this experiment." The men looked at each other and then back at me. They understood what I was telling them. "So, what are you going to do soldier?" I asked Bubba.

"Walk out the door and turn right, sir," Bubba said stone faced

"Why?"

"I have no intention of giving up a chance to be superman, sir."

I sighed and turned to Hosie, "And what are your intentions, soldier?"

Hosie took a moment and then said, "I intend to volunteer myself, sir."

"Why?"

"It will make me a better soldier for my country," Hosie said.

"You are dismissed," I said softer than I had intended.

The men walked to the door, opened it and turned right without hesitation.

Professor Matthew Ryan

Eve was 3-years-old when it first happened; prior to that, she was a normal child. Nothing was abnormal about her except her intelligence, independence and appetite. As normal a child as Eve appeared to be, I expected anomalies, it was only logically. Beyond the DNA in her from her mother and me, she contained the DNA from 38 species. I needed someone to watch over her when I went to work, at the same time, I was very aware that I was in Africa, where the paranormal in any shape and form would be classified as evil and my 3-year-old was unable to defend herself. So, I let technology do the work for me. I hooked up wireless sensors around her room. They sent a feed to my laptop, which helped me see exactly what she was doing. I taught two one hour classes in the mornings and evenings and after every class I quickly ran back home to check on her. While teaching my evening class on a Friday, I got a weird signal. I checked my laptop and the cameras were clouded. I couldn't see anything. I abruptly ran out of the class, got in my rickety blue Peugeot and drove to the house.

My neighbor's bulldog was barking at my house as though hell was in it. I opened the door and ran into the room, which seemed foggy. I walked in and, in the middle of the room, saw a translucent oval shaped cocoon that was 6 feet tall and 5 feet wide. In it, in the embryo position, was Eve. She seemed so peaceful. I touched the cocoon and it had a slimy feel on the outside. The next five inches felt like jelly and, after that, was something transparent and hard. Maybe it was intuition, but I didn't feel worried seeing her there. I put on classical music and began reading Charles Dickens' *Great Expectations* to her.

For two years, she remained in the cocoon state. I felt helpless watching her. The cocoon grabbed moisture from the air, so I knew that water was something that I could add to it. Therefore, three times every day, I poured a bucket of water over the cocoon. Between classes, I sat by the cocoon telling it fictional stories about trips we took around the world. The more I told the stories, the more real they felt to me. At one point, I literally believed that Eve and I were in Paris by the Eiffel Tower. I talked to her about everything, except where she came from. All she needed to know was that she was my daughter.

It was 6:47 in the morning one day when I heard noises in Eve's room. I quickly jumped out of bed and ran into her bedroom. There, I saw her, a towel wrapped around her, mopping the floor with a bucket of water. She was 4 feet 2 inches tall and skinny, a carbon copy of her mother. She even had her beautiful elegance.

"Is the roof leaking?" she asked, cleaning the fluid and white matter from the floor where her cocoon had been. I didn't say anything; I just looked at her in awe. "Daddy, is something wrong?" she asked.

I ran to her and squeezed her in my arms as I cried tears of joy. "Everything is perfect," I said. She kept looking at me as though I was crazy. She had no idea that for two years, she was in a cocoon. She believed that all the stories I told her were true and I tried to the best of my abilities to make them true.

***

At five, she could voluntarily create a webbed skin between her toes and fingers. She could also create a wing-like webbed skin from her elbow to her hips. When she asked me why, I told her that people were born with different bodily variations. Then, I reminded her that we were in West Africa where abnormal visuals scared people and that scared people did crazy things in fear.

At six, she could punch right through a deciduous tree. When she asked me why, I told her that God created some people stronger than the others and that with her strength, it was her responsibility to keep this gift to herself or God would be angry.

Prior to her seventh birthday, the hairdresser could braid her hair and do adventurous styles with it. However, after she turned seven, her hair became too strong for anyone to make changes to it, so it remained in like a permanent curly afro, which suited her perfectly. That year, she also learned that she could voluntarily change the color of her skin to blend with any background, like a chameleon. When she asked me why, I told her it had to do with a mutated chromosome in her system.

At this age, she seemed in control of herself and had begun school. Luckily, we were in a sea of black children and the country's xenophobia was negligible, so a white father with a black girl wasn't something that she was mocked for. Instead, it helped pull her up into the certain social circles.

By eight, she was agile, extremely fast, extremely flexible, and extremely smart. She wanted to get into sports and I had run out of lies, so I just told her "you know why you can't." She was so gracious about it. I was so happy with her ability to understand. She had known that I was lying, she didn't understand why, but she understood that it was enveloped in love. To fill the drum of lies, we went to Paris that Christmas.

At nine, she found herself sometimes comfortable sleeping upside down like a bat. Also, at night, her eyes glowed. She saw as clearly at night as she did during the day.

At 10, she could distinguish people as far as five miles away using sonar hearing and her ability to smell their scents.

By the time she was 11, there was a dead silence from any animal, including insects, whenever she was around. The dogs in the neighborhood fell silent and were amiable to her touch.

At 12, she began to get restless. She had to be active as her adrenaline was in high gear. She looked for any reason to get physical, running to the kitchen, jumping up onto the cupboards, doing hand stands with her fingers. Mental stimulation wasn't working. I couldn't keep her locked up from herself. I had prevented her from doing sports or even excelling publicly in her academics and I knew that I was heading toward a rebellion if I didn't give her an avenue through which to express herself. There was an isolated road by the university that ended in a path to the forest. We walked into the forest and I told her to do whatever she liked. I expected her to ask me what I meant, but, in a split second, she disappeared within the trees. She ran, climbed trees and jumped from branch to branch like a monkey. Her strength and agility was beyond belief. She kicked down trees with two inch diameters. I watched her for over three hours as she ran around the forest as though she was a child at Disneyland. If I hadn't told her to come back, she might have stayed there permanently. After that day, every week, we made it a point to go to a different woodland area in the state, so that she could run around. This decision seemed to help her restlessness.

At 15, Eve had grown to be the most beautiful child any father could want, both inside and outside, she was perfection for me to be around. She was 5 feet 9 inches tall and a little skinny. Her skin was as dark as her mother's skin and there was no sign of my DNA in her. Her character was flawless; everyone around her became infected by a dose of happiness that they lacked before they met her. The only thing that could give her away was her weight. For a skinny girl, she weighed 408 pounds.

In her entire existence, I never saw Eve lose her temper until the day after the country's Independence Day on October 2nd. My car broke down on our way back to the university campus from one of our weekly forest escapes. We were a mile away from our home, so Eve pushed the car to the side of the road. I tried calling the mechanic, but he didn't pick up his phone, with good reason as it was 10 at night. Two boys in a red corolla were driving drunk down the road, coming home from a party, singing at the top of their lungs. My paternal instincts kicked in and I put my hands around Eve's shoulders and we moved us as far away from the road as possible. The boys, in that moment, felt that it will be funny to give us a little scare, but the drunk driver didn't measure his swerve accurately. As he turned into us, the front of his car missed us by six feet, but the back of his car hit us. I used my body as a shield to protect Eve, while she quickly tucked her hand through my armpit and stopped the car's motion in its tracks. Her hand tore through the metal as she held the car in place. As soon as the car stopped, the boys looked at Eve and shocked at what they had done. When they saw that both of us were uninjured, they laughed out boisterously and drove off. That was the first time I saw her angry. Her eyes turned cat-like, something that looked like the quills of a porcupine, only larger as they were about three inches longer than those used by a hedgehog, jutted out of her arms, back and legs. Before I could hold her back, she made three incredible leaps over 40 feet high and landed on the trunk of their car. The magnitude of her landing caused the car to somersault backward in the air. In that split second, she looked back at me and she saw the horror in my eyes. Then, the real Eve took over. With the most impossible speed, while the car was rotating in midair, she jumped into it from the driver's window, grabbed both boys, yanked them through the passenger's side and dove out. The car landed thunderously on the road, it continuously spun sideways on the road crushing itself until it stopped totally wrecked.

The first of the drunken boys didn't seem to care about what had just happened. All he cared about was his car, which was completely totaled. He fell to his knees crying, "My father is going to kill me."

The other boy was passed out drunk beside the road. Eve and I disappeared quickly from the scene like we were never there, leaving our car behind. As much as I was sure the boys didn't believe what had happened, I knew that I couldn't take any chances, especially with all the blackberry cell phones floating around campus. Someone must have seen something. Eight days later, we were boarding a flight to Canada.

Ahmed Al-Harazi

Yemen is mostly a desert land; it is hot, humid and my home. I live in the center of the city of Sana'a, which is Yemen's largest city containing almost 1.1 million people. Shem, the son of Noah, formed the city but westerners can't stomach their history being rooted in an Arab settlement, so, instead, they call it a legend.

Due to the drone attacks, we, the anti-western brotherhood, realized that the best way to escape the American drones was to the stay in plain sight where their drone attacks would be seen by the entire world. Therefore, we were headquartered in a four story building in the center of the city. Most of the buildings around us were taller than ours, but the traditional structures were the same. Livestock roamed the stone-built ground floor. Children played on the staircase and the second floor held private living quarters for the families. We were on the topmost floor in the mafraj, a room where men meet in the afternoon. Large windows lined three walls of the room, forming a loggia.

With me were six, thickly bearded men carrying AK-47s. We all wore long robes and turbans. The men were my brothers; we lived and died for our faith. On the second floor the wives of the brothers were making arrangements for an upcoming wedding, while their children roamed from the third floor to the bottom floor. We had cleared the room of everything;

we didn't want anything to give away our identity. We placed curtains over the windows so that the only light in the room came from gas lamps. My name is Ahmed. I am a descendant of the Prophet Muhammad. I have to play the politics of the world during the day, while, under the cover of darkness, I plan attacks on westerners. It is my destiny; I have become the hand of god. Amongst us was an American convert, who joined us in our cause to destroy America. Sometimes, I doubted the authenticity of his faith in the words of the Prophet Muhammad. I believe he joined us so he could have three wives. He was formerly Bill Raines, but now he was Abubakar Abdu. He was 5 feet 3 inches tall, his brown hair stretched down to his shoulders, his beard extended past his chin and his brown eyes were buried under his red, tanned skin, burned from the Yemeni sun. I am 6 inches taller than him; my eyes and hair are both black. My hair and beard were neatly trimmed, something that I had to do to blend in with our enemies.

Abubakar set the camera on the tripod stand, as one of my armed brothers dragged and dropped the Yemeni employee from the United States embassy onto the floor. His hands and legs were tied behind him and his mouth was gagged. There was a black sack over his face. The man had on brown trousers and a blood stained, white long-sleeved shirt. The bleeding was the result of the occasional beatings we used to keep him under control in his hostage position. One of my brothers handed me a recently sharpened knife. I used my turban to cover my face, as did my brothers; we did not want our faces showing. Abubakar started recording.

Everyone stood behind me; the prisoner lay in front of me on the floor. I raised my knife and said, "An eye for an eye! You Americans have used your drones to kill our women and children and it's time for you to watch me cut the head of this man, so that you can see how we feel when one of your own bleeds."

The hostage began screaming and wiggling like a fish out of water, unable to talk or scream. I went down on my knees, took the sack of his head and put the knife by his neck. The man's eyes were wide open as the sharp blade touched his neck. He began moving, trying to get away. Three of my brothers held him in place.

"Watch the blood of your American brother-"

"Cut," Abubakar said, walking in front of the camera.

"What now?" I asked peeved.

"He is not American," Abubakar said frustrated.

"Okay, you can edit out that portion."

He took the turban off his face and sighed, "I know how these Americans think. We start cutting and they will think it was photo shopped. It has to be one take."

I stood up, angry, "Does this look like a joke to you?"

"Am I laughing?" he responded.

The man on the floor began crying. We ignored him. The other men got on their feet and folded their hands impatiently.

"You know what? You cut off his head and I will press record on the camera."

"Okay, I will do it," he said angrily.

In that second, something broke through the roof into the mafraj. Next, four inch thick nail-like objects spread across the whole room, hitting each of us. Then, I saw the figure. It ran across the wall perpendicular to us and grabbed the first gunman by the neck and flung him out the roof as though he was a sheet of crumbled paper. Two of my brothers opened fire on the demon, but it was so fast that none of their bullets touched him. Instead, his hands tore through their chests. The four of us who were still alive began firing blindly; the demon used my dead brothers as a shield and flung them with a magnitude that I couldn't fathom. The remaining four of us were thrown against the wall and fell to the ground. The demon pounced on the chest of one of brothers; its claws tearing into his chest. The demon was too fast to see, but my other brother had no intention of seeing it.

He broke through one of the windows and jumped to his death. Our hostage was on his knees praying to Allah. It was then that we saw the white-blond, blue-eyed western devil.

He was a teenage boy. I didn't see the claws that had been on his feet earlier. Instead, he looked normal. He spoke into a transmitter, "Ready for exit."

Abubakar fell on his knees, screaming, "I am an American citizen."

The boy squatted to him, "And I am god." He used the back of his hand to slap Abubakar; the force jolted Abubakar into the air. He broke through the wall and he died when his head separated from his spinal cord.

The embassy employee and I had coupled together in fear.

"Ahmed Al-Harazi?" the demon asked.

The embassy employee was quick to wiggle away from me, pointing his shaking fingers at me.

The six feet one demon walked over to the tied up embassy employee and I was positive he was going the eat him. The man's eyes widened even larger than when I had placed the knife on his throat. The white demon held him in place as claws grew out of his fingers. The embassy employee was about to scream but he quickly used his hands to hold his mouth shut. The demon used his claws to cut the man free. The man was quick to move away from the demon. What we had both seen, we couldn't forget. A rope fell through the ceiling into the room. Above it was a black hawk helicopter. The demon grabbed me by the arm and it felt like a two ton clamp had ahold of me. I immediately understood why one slap from the white demon could remove Abubakar's head.

He held on the rope and looked at the embassy employee, "Are you coming with us or are you using the stairs?"

The man spoke softly, almost as if he didn't want to vex the demon. "I...I... will use the stairs," he said.

The demon tugged on the rope and it pulled us into the helicopter.

Dr. Darshak Khurana

It had been a year since I had heard from my son. I patiently waited outside General Cole's office for over three hours as his uniformed secretary let everyone else in the office. I had on a blue suit. I wasn't as young as I used to be, my hair was now an equal mix of black and white. I had gained 15 extra pounds and my skin had wrinkled. Outside the general's office, it was freezing. There were four, straight-backed chairs against the wall outside the General's office.

I heard Cole laughing with the men who had walked passed me. I hadn't seen the man in five years. There was a time when his career had been in my hands, now I was no longer relevant. After Dr. Lin stole my methods and was able to replicate my serum, they were somehow able to brainwash Adam, making me obsolete. The only mystery was why they didn't kill me. Four years ago, I wished death upon myself when the army earned Adam's undivided loyalty. It took me until six months ago to realize that they had bugged every part of my house, car, clothes and shoes. They had literally built software that would help them determine the best way to relate to Adam. They used our daily interactions to get to him. The only thing was that I still couldn't say for sure what the best way was to relate to Adam. I treated Adam as a god, nothing more or less; that kind of affection couldn't be duplicated…at least, I hoped it couldn't.

A year ago, when on the verge of suicide, I met Marianne Gomez, a biochemist teaching at the University of Southern California. We met at the local library and, at first sight, I was blown away. Her lineage traced back to El Salvador; She was 45-years–old and had beautiful, full cheeks. She was my height with a smile that let you know that everything was alright. Her body was carved out of every man's desire. She was the lifeboat that kept me sane and the perfection of it all was that she loved me as I did her. In less than four months, I bought a house in California and we moved in together. She was always there to make me feel better when the sudden emptiness of the loss of Adam took over my thoughts.

"The General will see you now," the secretary said, robot-like without emotions, as the men in his office stepped out.

I walked into his office. He was seated behind his oak desk. Pictures of him and the last four presidents hung on the wall next to a large map of the world. On his desk sat a picture of him, his wife and his two sons, dressed in their army uniforms. The window was right behind him and allowed a view of the Washington monument. There were two chairs at the other end of the desk and at the other end of the room sat a brown couch. The office was smaller than I expected; it was about the same size as his waiting room. The man didn't seem to age; the only thing that gave away his age away was his hair. It was all white and, maybe, his muscles weren't as firm as they used to be.

"Darshak," he said stepping out from behind the desk and shaking my hand. "How are you doing?" Even though it had been years since we had seen each other, he still hated me. The fact that he called me by my first name unnerved me; it didn't sound good coming from his lips.

"I am fine," I said, trying to force a smile.

"Sit down. Relax," he said, literally pushing me down into a chair as he leaned on the table. "You did great things for your country."

"Nice to know someone acknowledges it."

"You know the nature of what you signed on for. None of us get credit for the work we do."

"Really, General, it's hard to keep count. Are you a one star general or is it two stars?"

"Darshak…" he said as he walked back around to his chair. "Darshak, Darshak, Darshak, with the money you made from Quad, Inc, you are practically a millionaire."

"I am a scientist! I want my name in history books. I deserve to be acknowledged," I protested.

"Then, you chose the wrong avenue to showcase your science," he said as if talking to a child.

"Why did you summon me here?" I asked angrily as I surveyed his pictures.

"I didn't summon you. I asked you to come over."

"You ordered me here," I said.

Power made him a happier man. He kept his composure as he pulled out a laptop, inserted a memory card and started a video. In it, I saw a car revolving in midair and then someone or something literally pulled two human beings from the car before it smashed. He turned the video off.

"Funny the things that you find on YouTube," he said.

"How does this concern me?" I asked, expecting a trick question.

"That was the same thing I wondered," he said as he leaned back in his chair, "but, you know how we are in the military, we always want everything perfectly in place, so we did a little investigating. It was uploaded by some theatre arts major with a Blackberry. Luckily for us, he saw the girl."

"It was a girl?" I asked.

"And her father. Now, what made the story stand out wasn't the fact that both father and daughter disappeared, neither was it the fact that she was black and the father was white, what stood out in our investigations," he stood and walked to the window, "was the fact that the girl was 15."

My face turned red, "Was it Ivan?"

"You mean the man formerly known as Ivan? The last time he was in Nigeria, he was Professor Matthew

Ryan. Now, he is probably someone else. We are in a post 9-11 era, tracking is easier now. We will find him."

"Is that why you brought me here?"

"You told me Adam was the only one possible."

"He was. Ivan must have figured out a way to-"

"To what!?" he screamed. Then, he sighed and said, "We boosted your ego. We understood that Ivan was the brains of the operation, but we played ignorant. You had one simple task, tap that man's mind and figure out what he was doing. After he was gone, nothing new came off you, but you looked me in the eye and told me that Adam could not be replicated except by cloning."

"Whatever that thing was, it's not Adam," I said. The room was cold, but I was beginning to sweat. The man I feared had resurfaced. "It's a shameful attempt at the perfection of Adam."

"Good day, Dr. Khurana," he said as he turned his back to me and looked out the window.

I stood there for as long as my pride would let me and then I asked, "Why am I still alive?"

"We are not barbarians," he said.

"I was with you on Mona Island."

He remained taciturn as he said, "Go home, Darshak."

"Is Adam okay?"

He ignored me. I needed to know, but I realized that there was a line that I couldn't cross. I took a deep breath and walked out of the room.

***

I arrived at LAX at noon and Marianne, my fiancée, was there to pick me up. We drove to our home in Toluca Lake. Along the way, I couldn't resist taking her hand and giving it kisses as we drove. She was good to me, necessary for any worth left in my existence. Our home in Toluca Lake was a traditional three bedroom, 2.5 bathroom bungalow. There was a three foot tall black gate around the house. Marianne had personally planted the colorful flowers at the front porch pillars. She also remodeled the chef's kitchen with stainless appliances, a carrera marble backsplash, designer stone countertops and custom cabinetry. She had created a fabulous flow to the dining area. Sunlight poured in through the windows onto the lush carpet and the fireplace. Further down the kitchen was the elegant, formal dining area and access to the backyard. In the dining area was an oval glass table with four chairs around it; it was a moderately small table as we hardly ever had guests. Outside, the covered patio provided room for leisure of all sorts and was surrounded by privacy-ensuring bushes. We loved our home and knew it was where we would spend the rest of our lives.

Marianne drove into the two car garage, closed the garage door and walked in through the door to the house, which led through the laundry room into the living room. I had my hands around her waist, giving her warm kisses on her neck as she giggled. She stopped when she saw someone sitting at our table, Adam. He wore a black, hooded shirt; a plain grey t-shirt and jeans. He was seated at one end of the table, had a glass of orange juice in front of him and had two other glasses, one beside him and the other opposite him.

"Adam," I said almost in tears as I ran to him. He got up and I hugged him. I turned to Marianne, "Marianne, Marianne," I said her name as though she couldn't see me. "This is my son. My boy has come home." They both shook hands.

"Your father has told me so much about you," Marianne said.

"He is not my father," Adam replied insouciantly as he sat back down and continued drinking his orange juice. Marianne gently held my hand, as I stood with her awkwardly. "The both of you should sit. I have two glasses of orange juice set out for you."

I whispered to Marianne, "Why don't you go get things together in the room. I will come join you soon?"

"No," Adam said. "We all will sit around this oval table and drink our orange juice."

"I don't hear from you for a year, not even an email, and when you come home, you start barking orders," I yelled as the angry father I was.

"I wasn't barking," he said as he looked back at me, reminding me of the animal he could become.

"Marianne, please leave me alone with my son," I said.

"Your son? I am no longer your god?" Adam asked.

"I searched for you. I begged everyone to find you, to tell me that you were okay and this is how you choose to stomp on the affection of your father."

Adam sipped on his orange juice, "I have a story to tell and Marianne will be very interested in it."

"It's okay," she said holding my hand. She sat opposite Adam. I sat down next to him, peeved.

"The restart program," Adam began.

"Adam!" I jumped in, standing up.

"Sit down," he said with an empyrean authority. I saw the transparent, three inch thick nail-like quills stand out from his hands, tearing through his clothing, a sign that he was truly mad. Fear, not only for me, but for Marianne as well, drove me back down into my seat. However, Marianne seemed composed as she watched him. She didn't understand that if he told her too much, she will be compromised; a perfect specimen for accidental death. Adam was issuing her death warrant with clandestine words.

"Please, Adam, don't," I begged him, trying to look into his eyes, which were set on Marianne.

"The restart program was a serum basically created to upgrade a human to the best that he could be. From the experiments that they conducted, they knew that there was one major side effect, insomnia. So, when the two soldiers volunteered, they decided to put them in sleeping chambers. But there was a problem," he paused as he took a sip of his orange juice. I was breathing hard; hatred was evident through the tears that squeezed through my eyes as I looked at this creature I loved like a son. "The soldiers were very active. The serum didn't make them stronger or faster, it only made them work like hell to be the best that their bodies could be. They worked like animals, 24 hours a day to be the best that they could be. Their cardio was inhuman. They built their strength, speed and gun precision to perfection. The best part was that their sensory cortex thalamus didn't allow them to feel fear anymore; they were fearless. Now, the only problem was that beyond the sleeplessness, their testosterone levels went straight through the roof, increasing their sexual proclivity, making it dangerous for anyone of the opposite sex to be around them. Also, there was something about the two men being together in the same room that led to the most vicious physicality. On more than one occasion they almost killed each other. Eventually, they had to literally separate them by state lines. Then, with the data they had, they decided to try the experiment on 25 women and 25 men. Fifteen days after they received the serum, the women killed themselves. The 25 men were okay for the first year and, then, they began attacking each other, which resulted in two deaths. The others had to be separated and the military found themselves using their resources to prevent these men from hunting each other down. That suddenly became their single most important goal," Adam said as he finished the orange juice in his glass. Then, he walked to fridge, got out another carton of orange juice, brought it back to the table, filled his glass, took a sip and sat down. He was enjoying the fact he held us hostage with his presence.

Marianne, on the other hand, quietly watched him, not a trace of emotion was on her face.

He continued. "Soon, five years had passed and the military needed their merchandise working together; individually they weren't as powerful. Now, as the original tests were only administered to lab rats, which lived for two to three years, nobody knew what would happen after that. However, year five was when the magic started happening. The body is such a powerfully adaptable creation that it's mind blowing," he said as he made an explosive gesture with his hands.

At this point, I was interested in knowing what was going on with my serum; I had been shut out after they had tested it on the first two soldiers.

He continued, "Their bodies began to develop ZZ and ZW chromosomes." He was talking like a scientist; he was talking like me. He was talking like my son. "Their testosterone levels dropped and their estrogen levels went way up. The soldiers began to change. They suddenly began sleeping on their own. They could now work together. They became very strong and there was only one problem, which wasn't really a problem...in the right situation." He smiled at Marianne. "The men became women, everything in their body changed to that of a woman." He put his index finger to his lips. "Yes, every single part of them. Am I right, Hosie? Are you now all woman?" I looked from Adam to Marianne confused.

Before I knew what was going on, with the speed of nothing human, Adam jumped across the table and swung me around him as a bullet pierced through the window into the chair I was sitting in. Marianne kicked her chair at Adam, rolled on the ground to the kitchen cabinet and pulled out two semi-automatic handguns from underneath the sink. I laid on the floor in awe, unsure of what was happening. She fired at Adam, who bounced from left to right like a wild cat, but faster. He escaped the avalanche of bullets and grabbed Marianne's hands. When he twisted them, she let go of the guns and kicked him in the chest. The force threw him onto the floor, but, like a cat, he sprung back up. She immediately launched a howitzer of punches, which he dodged. Then, he grabbed her by the neck and slammed her so hard into the ground that she broke the foundation. Bullets from machine guns began spraying the house. Adam quickly rolled like a ball toward me and grabbed me. I found myself enveloped within him like a child in a tire as he rolled.

We broke out of the back door, rolled through the backyard and into the street. He dropped me there and said, "Give me 10 minutes and I will be back."

I held his hand, "What are you going back for?"

"I have to kill them or you will be dead within the hour," he said. Then, he sped back into the house. I heard three more shots and then dead silence. He came out in four minutes and 37 seconds. "Steal a car and drive. Toss a coin, let the face of the coin determine any major turn you take while driving. Whatever happens, make sure you keep on driving."

"How will you know where I am?" I asked worried.

"If I know where you are, then they will know where you are," he said. Then, he disappeared, without even saying goodbye.

General Coriolanus Cole

I slept in the office a lot, especially when there was an emergency. Sleep was a weakness, but a necessity to keep one recharged. I turned off the light and lay on the brown couch in my office. With everything going on, I knew that it was pointless leaving the office because some emergency situation would bring me back. It was 2:29 AM; armed soldiers secured the parameter outside the office and building. My office was on the third floor of the three story building. The glass outside the building was tinted in order to prevent anyone from looking in. On the couch, I thought of all of the things that I could do better for my country. The cyber-attacks were now taking precedence over the real, physical terrorists who were planning every day to attack us just because of the freedom of the red, white and blue. In that moment, my instincts kicked in. I opened my eyes to find Adam standing over me. I bounced up, alarmed. I knew that was what he wanted, so I sat up on the couch and he sat by me quietly.

"Were they asleep on duty?" I asked.

"No, they were pretty alert. With their general in the office, they were in holding their posts diligently," Adam said looking straight ahead instead of at me.

"How many were there?"

"I counted 12. There might be more in the building."

"And not one of them saw you enter a secured zone?" I asked, smiling, genuinely impressed.

His face remained stiff as he said, "We had a deal, Coriolanus?"

"I kept my end."

"You had him sleeping with a trans-human soldier."

"The politically correct terminology is T-soldier. It's still maximum clearance to be privy to that kind of information."

"You had him sleeping with a trans-human soldier," he repeated.

"He was a wreck when you left him for us. I didn't trust his sanity. I didn't want him doing something stupid, so I had Hosie watch him."

"You had Hosie... or Marianne as he called her... watch him, waiting for him to make a mistake, so that she could kill him."

"It's the nature of our job."

"We made a deal, Coriolanus. If you didn't touch a hair on him, then I was all yours."

"Nobody touched him and nobody would have. He was happy. He wasn't going to do anything stupid and you knew that. You went in there to create chaos because..." I stood, watching his expressionless face and I smiled, "you were jealous. You wanted him miserable. You needed him miserable. That's the only way you felt attached to him." He sat taciturn looking forward. I leaned against the wall. "For a year, you could have gone to visit him, but you chose not to. You cut him off and then you suddenly returned and killed the woman he loved."

"He was a man," Adam said.

"Not to him. She had a vagina and that was all the woman he needed to know."

"What if you're right?"

"I know I'm right."

He looked at me with his catlike eyes, "What makes you so sure that this isn't one of the last moments of your life?"

I laughed, "You need Darshak because he is your loyal disciple. You need me because I am the only one who can let you be what you really are and have the greatest country in the world appreciate you for it."

"I can take on the greatest country in the world."

"Don't be ludicrous, Adam. We have DNA seeking missiles, heat seeking missiles, drones and, if by some crazy miracle you take over a town, we have nukes. Not to mention the 25 T-soldiers."

"22."

"You killed 3 of them!?" Now, I was really angry.

"What was I supposed to do with them? Spank them? They engaged me first."

"You could have broken their legs or something. Those soldiers cost us a fortune to nurture and get to their perfect states."

"Then, you need to tell them to back off when they see me coming. Anyway, one survived."

"Hosie?"

"No."

"Which one?"

"I don't know. Those ugly trannies all seem alike to me."

"You had a problem with Hosie. I can live with that, but killing two, damn it, Adam!" I marched to my desk. "Do you think this is all a joke?" I screamed.

A soldier ran into the room, "Is everything okay, sir?"

"Get out!" I screamed at the soldier and he immediately left. "You know what we've been through to get these soldiers to their present states?"

Adam laughed, "I finally found your kryptonite... money."

"What do you think a general does? The Patton era of glory is behind us. It's now money management."

"There was a time when you cared about your men," Adam said. I knew he was referring to the incident on Mona Island. I couldn't defend my actions then or many of my actions after that.

"When you have legions of men under your command, it's difficult to keep track of every one of them," I said as I leaned against my desk. "Promise me that you won't kill any more of the T-soldiers."

"If they engage me, I will kill them. If they don't, then they will live."

"You realize that they are at a point where they have symbiotic bond, right? You killed three of them; they know and they will come for you."

"Let them come."

"Lucky for you, for some divine reason, their loyalty to me comes before anything else."

"Lucky for me," he said sarcastically.

"Let me rephrase that. Promise me that you won't provoking any of the T–soldiers now that you know that's their weakness," I said as I looked him in the eyes.

"I will try."

I sighed; it was the best I would get from him. "We found Professor Kozlov in Canada. We need you to capture him and bring him here."

"And if I refuse?"

"Then, we might have to start tracking down Darshak." I put my hand to my head and laughed. "Can you believe that a man as smart as he is actually used the ATM in Arizona three hours ago when he is supposed to be on the run?"

"He has to eat."

"You want me to go hold his hand, bring him back and tell him everything is going to be alright?" I asked, still laughing.

"Nah, let him keep running. It will get him in shape," Adam said as he headed toward my office door. He stopped by the door. "It's interesting that you said 25 T-soldiers."

"What's interesting about that?"

"You always underestimate me, Coriolanus. That's the kind of thing that will get you killed."

"What type of general would I be if I don't have any secrets?"

"Say hi to the hermaphrodites," he said as he kept his focus on me. I didn't give anything away; I just looked back at him, "My bad, they are women now."

"And your point is...?"

"Three things, Coriolanus...," as he spoke, he studied my facial expression, trying to read my physiognomy. "Doctor Lin... Sloane... and the Chameleons."

I smiled. "First thing that my father told me when I held my first gun was that a fool thinks he knows everything, a wise man knows he knows nothing... Be wise, Adam." I watched his mind work. There was so much that I could tell him to hurt him or maybe help him, but, for now, I had no idea if the information shared with him was to the advantage of the Chameleon Project or a liability.

He abruptly headed out the door and disappeared from my line of view.

Senator Dakota Knox

Father died of a heart attack at the age of 89. Before his death, he played a crucial role in getting me elected as a member of the house of representative and then as the junior senator of Texas. He even picked the man I married, Bradley Connery, who was everything I needed in a husband, good-looking and weak. The church funeral was three–quarters full. It was quick and to the point. At eight, we converged in his office at his Texas ranch. In the room, Reagan, my older brother, stood with Brenda, his 41-year-old curly brunette wife who looked 10 years his senior; Krystal, my father's 25-year-old bride; and his lawyer, Jake Holmes. Bradley wasn't mentioned in the will, so it was pointless for me to let him stay and listen to anything that didn't concern him. Father's lawyer was a 62-year-old, five–foot, three inch tall, white male with a toupee on his head. His belly sat six inches in front of his chest and his thick, white moustache almost covered his upper lip. He always had a cigar between his lips. The logs in the fireplace were crackling; the weather wasn't cold and why anyone decided to get a fire started was a mystery to me. We sat on two couches that faced each other, and they rested on old, historic plank floors. The walls were cream-colored and French double doors led into the room.

Jake Holmes read the will, while standing between the two couches with a cigar in his hand. At the beginning of his will, father went on a loquacious spill about how he worked to get where he was and talked about all of the things that he had suffered to get the fortunes he amassed. I had to listen to his babble for close to 15 minutes, pretending that I empathized with his struggles, while I knew that the man was a thug who had the blood of innocent people on his hands. Brenda was wailing like a goat, crying for a man she hated as much as he couldn't stand her. He forbade Reagan from bringing his wife anywhere near him in public. His words were, "I don't want anyone connecting her ugliness to my family." Father had a devilish sense of humor. Now, Krystal, on the other hand, was a girl who worked hard for her money, kissing and holding hands with the wrinkled old man; she was a trooper. The lawyer finally got to the meat of things. He gave Brenda a dollar and, then quoting the will, said, "That is what you are worth and I am being generous." I tried not to smile. She immediately stopped her crocodile tears and, with a deep frown, leaned back against the couch and crossed her legs, while her husband held her hand. To his young bride, he gave his $400,000 Deep Impact Yacht, his houses in Monaco and Beverly Hills and $25 million. Then, the Jerry Springer show began.

"Is that it?" Krystal asked the lawyer in her shrill voice, taking the veil off her face and the black hat off her head. She was wearing a black dress that showed her hour glass figure. With her black high heels on, she was about five foot nine inches tall.

"For you," the lawyer said, "yes."

Standing up calmly, she said, "How can I be sure that this will isn't a forgery?"

"It was signed in the presence of witnesses and a notary."

"I gave that man my youth, six of the best years of my life and all I get is $25 million, a boat and two houses?" she asked, losing her composure. Reagan and I looked at each other, not sure if we should be laughing. "You haven't heard the last of me. You'll be hearing from my lawyer," she said as she stomped out of the room, slamming the door behind her.

The lawyer continued reading as though nothing out of the ordinary had happened. "To my children, Reagan and Dakota, you've both made me proud in everything you've done, except one thing. Reagan, my son, I believe myself to be a modern father and I've never told you who to date, but the only demand I ever asked of you was simple, do not marry that Brenda girl. Yet, you chose to do it. She came with a dying company that we had to bail out and didn't bring anything to the table that would make me proud of her. You bribed your way back into my affections with my two grandchildren and, for them, I forgave you, but I did not forget. Dakota, you are no spring chicken and you have not given me any grandchildren; not one that I could hold. I even got you a husband and you still refused to extend my immortality. For that, I will never forgive you. So, this is my will, Dakota will control all of my remaining assets with full carte blanche, until Reagan's children turn 18 and then everything goes to them. This is my last will and testament."

Reagan and I looked at each other with our mouths open; there was an evil gleam in Brenda's eye.

The lawyer sighed, waiting for some form of response from the two of us. When he didn't get any, he said, "I'm thirsty. I need something to drink." Then, he headed out the door.

Brenda quickly said, "I'll join you." She followed him to the living room, leaving us alone.

"That perverted old bastard," Reagan said.

"You can say that again," I said as I laid flat on the couch, using my hand to massage my forehead. "I knew that he would find some way to screw us."

"Easy for you to say; he left me with nothing. Brenda, at least, got a dollar." I laughed. "It's not funny, Dakota."

"Sorry," I said.

"I got nothing from the old bastard; you're already a senator and, still, he gives you my job," he said.

"About that," I sat up straight, "let's face it, it would be awkward you and I to work together and have you report to me. You aren't really thinking of coming back, are you?"

He looked at me, awed, "Are you firing me?"

"No, no, no, Reagan," I sat up and put my hand on his knee. "I am retiring you."

"You selfish-"

"No name calling, Reagan. Its business, nothing more."

"You are a senator, for goodness sake. You don't have the time to deal with this."

"True, that's what consultants are for," I said.

He abruptly stood. I could see it in his eyes, he was contemplating strangling me. I was getting my lungs ready to scream; there were a lot of people in the house who would come save me if he tried anything barbaric. He sighed, laughed to himself and headed toward the door.

"No hard feelings," I said.

He looked back at me, "Julius turns 14 in August. You, by now, should know that time flies when you're getting older." He grinned and continued, "Four Years ago, we bought a casino in Las Vegas and now the casino is making us a bundle. In about the same time, Julius will take over and we will kick you into the streets." He marched out of the room.

What fascinated me the most was the idea that I would make minced meat out of his two children before they turned 18 didn't even cross my brother's mind. It was puzzling how anyone could believe that someone who has power would just give it away.

Adam

Humanity is a fallacy. It's pathetic when humans think they are anything, but animals. It's incredible when that they believe themselves to be above animals; animals kill for food, humans kill for religion, sex, power and, in desperate situations, each other for food. I hate them and everything about them. They see the world only from their eyes; the good ones are very few, but the bad ones are quick to announce their goodness.

I was standing outside a modern, simple, spacious cabin on a remote 20 acres up in the Blue Mountains in Ontario, Canada. The cabin was hidden in the middle of a thick forest; a quarter of a mile away was the most beautiful panoramic view of the mountains. The cabin was made of two sections, a tall tower and a lean-to area. The lean-to section was elevated and contained the main living area. There was a loft in the living area as well as two bedrooms. The cabin's structure was fitted by two glulam beams. The house was moved to its present location. The floor space was about 1,040 square feet and the roofing style was conventional. The walls and the floor were battened. There was a large bedroom at the bottom of the tower and a 16 foot spiral staircase that led to the top of the tower.

It was the kind of place that I would love to live in, trees to hop on, space to run without these nosy humans. It was my kind of place, isolated with enough space for me to be me. I had on a black, hooded sweatshirt and blue jeans. I wasn't cold, but I didn't want to stand out if anyone happened to be passing by. Canada was an ally to the United States so the army's transportation of me to the location had to be orthodox.

I stood outside the cabin; there was a different smell around the area. It wasn't human or animal, it was something different, something familiar, but I couldn't put my finger on it. No one was in the house and, for some ungodly reason, I couldn't enter. It was almost as though something had pissed around it, marking it as its territory. I wasn't scared. I couldn't be scared as nothing of this planet scared me…maybe it wasn't of this planet. I was intrigued by this discovery, but, what fascinated me the most was my reaction. I was, for the first time, cautious.

I heard his truck coming. He was about 10 miles away and I could smell him. People's scents were signatures that became tattooed in my memory. I have to admit that it was pretty awesome because the last time I saw the man was the day I was born. Five miles away, he stopped the truck and I began to wonder if he knew that I was there. I patiently waited at the front of his house for his next move. If he drove away, I had to do this the hard way; run after him, catch him and bring him in.

He remained in the same spot for 25 minutes. I wasn't sure what to do. If he knew that I was there, he would be running; it was the typical human response. Instead, he remained in the same spot. If he were closer to me, I would have been able to feel the vibrations of his heartbeat and sense his fear. I squatted down and picked up an igneous rock. I crushed it into tiny particles. I was getting impatient. The man knew I was here. He wanted me to run to him, but why? I am proud, but not stupid. Anyone who knows fear and doesn't run from it is either mad or knows how to contain it. The truck began moving toward the house, which began to mess with my train of thought. I began debating whether I should hide and surprise him or just attack him. However, my train of thought took longer than I wanted and his truck pulled up in front of me.

He stopped the Ford F-150 truck and looked out the window. "Can I help you?" he asked. The man had a thick, sand and pepper beard, his hair was askew and his grey sports jacket was designed for a much smaller man. He didn't recognize me.

"Yes, you can," I replied.

He remained in the driver's seat and looked at me as though I was insane. "Well, young man, how can I help you?"

This day was embarrassing and time consuming and I just wanted to get it over with, so I decided to make a grand entrance. I leapt into the air and landed with the weight of the Earth through the windshield of his car. As the glass shattered, he shielded himself and only received a few cuts on his face. I sat in the passenger's seat as though I had come in through the door.

"Professor Ivan Kozlov," I said as he looked back at me in horror. "My name is Adam and I am here to take you home." The man's heartbeat was as fast as a humming bird's heartbeat. The stench of fear was priceless to someone like me. "Well...?" I asked. He still had the look of horror on his face. In a split second, it hit me; he wasn't afraid of me, he was afraid for me.

Abruptly, something crashed onto the roof of the truck. I looked up, bewildered. Then, two hands tore through the metal roof, grabbed my neck and arm like gigantic clamps and, with a demonic force, pulled me up, completely tearing open the roof of the truck. Then, it flung me into the forest. My momentum broke four thick trees before I landed, face first, onto the ground. I must have lost consciousness for about two seconds. I woke sharply to a punch with the weight of 3,000 pounds behind it. The pain was excruciating and the force dug me deep into the ground. I didn't know what type of demon I was dealing with. Claws grew out of my fingernails and I dug a deep burrow into the Earth as fast as a badger, as far away from the creature as I could. To my greatest horror, the demon chased me into the ground. I dug my way back to the surface and waited for it. I had caught my breath. I was ready for it. I wasn't afraid. I was ready. I had to be ready. After 10 seconds, I knew that something was wrong. Why wasn't it coming out of the ground? I bent down and placed my hand on the ground. Then, I put my ear to the ground and was punched in the jaw. I flew into the air backward. I felt the weight of the creature on me. I curled my head, hands and feet revealing only my back like a turtle, protecting myself as the titan punched me in the back of my head and ribs. Then, I heard a scream.

"Eve!"

Instantly, the attack stopped. I saw Professor Kozlov ten feet away, sweating from running toward us.

I used that split second to get back on my feet and I saw the creature for the first time. She was the most beautiful thing that I had ever seen. She had ebony skin and curly black hair. She was a little skinny at 5 foot 9 inches tall. I was a little bewildered that this skinny, black girl weighed close to a ton. She had on a skin–tight pair of blue jeans and a public enemy t-shirt.

"You can run back home, unless you are hungry for more," she said, her voice so calm that she sounded like a shrink. I detected an African accent.

I stretched my neck and arms, "I'm just getting warmed up, little girl."

She turned toward the professor, who gave her a sign of approval. Like lightning, she was by my side attempting to punch me. I defended her colossal attacks and threw back some of mine, which she deflected until I managed to kick her fully in the chest, a move that knocked her to the ground.

With a smile, I said, "I'm sorry. Did that hurt?"

She got up and smiled, "A little."

"I am not accustomed to attacking pretty girls," I said.

"You think I'm pretty?" she asked overdramatically, being sarcastic.

"Don't overdo it," I said, peeved that she was mocking me.

"Now, let's get this started," she said, bouncing around like a boxer.

She leaped up into the air and came toward me. I sprung up a tree as she landed forcefully on the spot where I had been standing. I jumped on her back and attempted to choke her, but I wasn't fast enough. She grabbed my arm and flung me wickedly to the ground. Then, she kicked me away by my head as though I was a soccer ball. It took me a moment to regain my senses. Then, a headache hit me and I massaged my head.

"You can cry; there is no shame in it," she said as she stood between two trees.

"Enough, Eve," the professor said.

"Is that all you've got?" I asked.

She looked back at the professor, who was getting frustrated. I took advantage of that distraction and swiftly kicked her in the ribs, sending her flying into several trees. I rushed to her to finish the job, but she leaped up into the air. I jumped after her, webbed skin grew from her elbow to her waist, tearing through her t–shirt, allowing her to glide down the mountain. I chased after her, my webbed skin also tearing through my clothing. She moved through the air like a bat, but I was on her. I knew that she was recuperating from my hit and I wanted to take advantage before she got her full strength back. I tried to shoot out my quills at her as we glided through the air, but nothing came out. There was something about the similarity between us that prevented the spikes from working on her. The cold wind blew harshly on me as I chased after her.

If she was like me, then her body regenerated when hurt and it did so quickly, so I had to catch up to her. Unfortunately, I realized that it had taken me too long to catch up to her when she suddenly turned in midair and began gliding toward me with the full wind behind her. It happened faster than I could comprehend and she was on me in mid-air, pounding me with those 3,000 pound punches, the weight of which threw me into the side of the mountain. She wasn't done with me. She flung off her shoes off; hair grew out of her feet and claws grew out from her toenails. She used them to clamp onto the mountain with me between her legs. She used her left hand to steady me vertically against the mountain 450 feet above sea level, while her right hand began pounding away at me. After the first strike to my face, I weakly attempted to defend her next punches. After the second strike to my ribs, I didn't have any energy left with which to defend myself. After the third strike to my chest, I was praying for the professor to scream for her to stop. After the fourth punch, I lost consciousness.

***

There was a peaceful calm to my present state; there was nothing in my head, nothing to worry about, nothing to think of and nothing that mattered. I was in a state of peaceful nothing and I knew this was perfection to a creation like me, but I had to leave it in order to find out where she was from, who she was and, most importantly, what she was. I opened my eyes and found myself naked in the embryo position, floating in an oval-shaped, transparent cocoon with a six foot diameter. The outer walls were like jelly and there was fluid in the center that was made of water absorbed from the atmosphere and my waste products. The smell in the cocoon was disgusting and I immediately busted out of it, the fluid from the cocoon spilling across the garage. I stood shivering before walking over to the wooden garage door and opening it. The sun hit my naked body. The light was a little too harsh, so I covered my eyes. I saw my clothes hanging by the door and quickly donned them. I was standing outside a standalone 10 by 10 foot garage. I saw the cabin a half mile away and walked toward it, unsure of why I was still alive. During the walk, I began debating whether I was actually dead.

Once outside the cabin, I could see her in the kitchen, beside the loft, cooking. I suddenly felt embarrassed. I had been literally beaten unconscious by this girl, this perfect recreation of me. The cabin had a battened patio, six wooden steps from the ground. Then, a sliding door led to the loft. There was a small window in the kitchen, so that someone in the kitchen could easily see who was at the door. I knew she knew I was by the door, but she chose to ignore me, doing whatever she was doing in the kitchen. If she hadn't shown me her barbaric strength, I would have probably kicked open the door. However, I knew that I had to be careful with her; the girl was an untamed creature. After waiting for a moment for her to acknowledge me, I realized it was pointless playing her teenage games and I knocked.

"Well, well, well. If it isn't sleeping beauty," she said with her uncultured cynical tone.

I attempted a forced smile, "Hello."

She didn't look my way. She had something new on, a white, long-sleeved t-shirt and dungarees.

"There is a bucket and mop by the side of the house. Take it and clean your filth from the garage," she said as she continued cutting her vegetables.

It didn't make sense to me. Here I was trying to be cordial and she was talking to me as though I was her maid. "You realize that you're a rude, little girl, right?"

She stopped cutting and looked at me straight in the eye, "Really?" she asked.

"I understand that you can't help it. It's just your nature," I said.

"Are you trying to annoy me?" she asked, putting her head through the small window. "You, of all people, know what I do to people who make me angry."

"What happened was a fluke," I responded.

She scoffed and continued cutting her vegetables, so I realized that I had to give her a more credible defense.

"I always take my time attempting to understand my enemies the first time around. If we were to engage now, I would be ready."

"Sure, you are," she said, sarcastically.

"Stop doing that."

"Doing what?"

"Mocking me."

"And if I don't? What are you going to do about it?"

I took a deep breath. I was angry, very angry, but, after what happened with her, I knew better than to physically confront her. The animal she was, she was probably longing for another fight. "You are very mean," I said instead. After the words came out of my mouth, I realized how weak it made me feel and shamelessly vulnerable that someone as powerful as myself could let this little girl humble me.

The words took her by surprise. She attempted to throw back a witty remark, but the words kept getting lodged in her throat. She curled her lips, marched out of the kitchen and through the main door until we were face-to-face. "You're calling me mean!? Me? Mean!? You came to our home to kill my father and you have the audacity to call me mean."

"You're getting ahead of yourself. I didn't come here to kill Professor Kozlov."

"Right," she said in her mocking tone. "You just came here to talk chemistry."

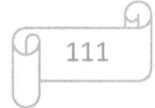

"Well… I came here to kidnap him."

Then, the weirdest thing happened. I realized that I had never had to lie in my life; it had never been necessary against inconsequential mortals. Those weren't the words that I wanted out of my mouth, but those were the words that came out.

"Now, that makes everything all better."

"Nobody told me about you."

"Shame on them for not telling you that Professor Kozlov had a daughter. You-"

"Stop calling him your father!" I said louder than I expected.

She looked at me for a second before she replied, "By the mountain, I bashed you over 25 times after you got unconscious and then I let your body drop all the way to the ground. I still remember the thump that your body made when it crashed to the ground. I smiled when I left you to die... My father screamed at me and ordered me to bring your body back up the mountain. I carried you here, hoping you were dead, but, unfortunately, your body began regenerating and creating a cocoon. The moral of the story is this…next time I want you dead, I will remove your head from your body. So, if you ever tell me what to do again, you know now what I will do. Do you understand me?"

I looked at her, bewildered by her beauty and scared at the same time.

"Do you understand me?"

I was a little surprised that she didn't catch the reality of our situation.

"There are only two of us who exist in the entire world. My name is Adam and you are Eve. You and I are going to create the perfect species on this polluted planet. Our offspring might have to mingle with these pathetic humans, but when our generations are enough in numbers, they will band together and wipe every single one of these humans from the planet, so that a more deserving species can rule."

She looked at me expressionless.

I looked into her eyes and said, "We are one."

Moving 75 miles an hour, her hand hit me and began crushing my throat. In that time, I caught the scent of Professor Kozlov, so did she and she let me go. "When father comes, thank him for your life and get out. Never come here again or, I swear, I will kill you this time."

Professor Kozlov drove to the front of the cabin in his truck. It was impressive how quickly they got the truck fixed, it looked even better than the last time I saw it. He got out of his truck smiling ear to ear when he saw me. The man literally ran out of his car to meet me. "Adam…," he said touching my face. Normally, I would have slapped his head from his body, but Eve didn't lose sight of me for a second. "Eve, you are not alone. You are not alone, my dear" he said joyfully as tears welled up in his eyes. "Come, come, come," he said, opening the door. "You must be famished. Eve is the greatest cook on the planet," he said, very proud of her.

"Stop it, daddy," she said. The professor made her happy. I wasn't comfortable with that. "Unfortunately, father, he said that he had to leave and, you know what… I will let him tell you." She turned to me and gestured for me to repeat her initial command.

"I would love to stay and have Eve's scrumptious dinner," I said. If looks could kill, I would have died just from the way that Eve looked at me. She was literally counting the seconds until the moment when she could decapitate me.

"Good, good, good," he said as he put his hand on my shoulder, ushering me into their loft. I turned to Eve and grinned at her frowning face.

The dining area was very intimate with a small, round, wooden table with two chairs. There were pictures of Eve and the professor all over the walls. The room was a little tight, but, in the context of homeliness, it worked. The man sat beside me and peered at me as an art lover would examine a Van Gogh painting.

"So, Adam, tell me, how many times have you entered the cocoon state?" Kozlov asked, with Eve 20 paces away by the refrigerator in the kitchen.

She took out a frozen chicken, placed it on a cutting board and began cutting, her eyes focused on me with a stern expression on her face.

"This was my second time," I said.

"So, your body uses the cocoon state to heal itself," Kozlov said more to himself than to me. "The first time you were in the cocoon state, how long did it last?"

"A year," I responded. Kozlov looked back at Eve and they seemed to have a speechless agreement between the two of them. "So, big deal, she spent two years as a cocoon and I spent one year."

"How did you know that?" Kozlov asked, bewildered.

"I can understand her thoughts," I replied. "The same way she and I can understand the thoughts of any animal around us. The same way any two animals can understand each other without making sounds to each other."

"Telepathy," Kozlov said.

Eve stabbed the knife into the chopping board, loud enough to command the attention in the room. "Chce cie zabic," she said in Polish.

I translated it in my head, "He wants to kill you."

"On jest nas'zym gosciem," the professor replied.

I again translated it the professor's reply to mean, "He is our guest."

Then I said, "For the record, I just wanted to kidnap him, not kill him," I cut in.

"Shut up!" she screamed at me.

Kozlov looked at her, bewildered. "Forgive my daughter; she isn't comfortable with things that she doesn't understand."

"But she is not your daughter," I said.

The genteel expression that he had on his face disappeared and was replaced by reserved anger. I could see Eve waiting for an opening to strike at me, if her father would let her. "Why would you say that?" he asked.

I had to be smart and share a believable observation, "You are white. She is black."

"Uh huh," Kozlov said, the smile returning to his face. "You're a racist."

"I'm not a racist," I said.

"It pretty much sounds that way to me," Eve said as she mixed her vegetables and chicken into a pot.

"We are not judgmental. Frankly, I respect an open racist a lot more than one who pretends to believe in equality and then goes on the internet to be his true racist self," Kozlov said as though sharing a theory.

"I am not a racist!" I lost my temper for a split second, causing the quills to spike out of my skin. However, the oddest thing happened, the professor did not react in fear, neither did Eve attempt to shield him. It was as though I was an angry toddler among adults. "I don't believe in equality. I believe that Eve and I are the next stage of evolution. We are not like your degenerated human species."

The professor took the moment seriously. He imposed his gaze on mine and then turned to Eve. They burst out laughing. I wasn't amused. I was being mocked. I, who am treated as a god by the greatest military force in the world, was being mocked by these human. I immediately stretched out my hand to clamp the stupid man's throat, but Eve, with that mind blowing speed, was by me to grab my arm. She flung me down onto the ground, while, simultaneously, landing a 2,000 pound punch into my belly for good measure. My body dented the floor when I landed. Eve stood by her father, ready for another fight.

"Anyone want some tea?" Kozlov asked, walking to the kitchen.

I stood up with Eve's gaze on me. "Your punch feels much lighter," I said. She ignored her father.

"It's the cocoon. It regenerates your body to make it stronger, able to absorb more and give more power. It also increases your speed," Kozlov said as he made herbal tea. Eve watched me like a hungry lioness hunting a deer.

"I wasn't going to hurt him. I just wanted him to stop laughing at me," I said, not out of fear, but more to build an understanding with her.

"She knows. She is just a little possessive of her father," Kozlov said as though I was talking to him. He walked back to the table and kissed her on the cheek. She let her guard down. "Now," he said sternly as though we were in the middle of an intense dialogue. "The reason we laughed is because your DNA is virtually human. The only difference is due to the infusion. Your chromosomes were juggled around perfectly, in comparison to us. The other animal DNA inclusions just helped to fortify the nucleosome positioning. Think about it. There are barely any DNA variations between man and chimps or dogs; it's just the arrangement. You and Eve basically have the perfect DNA structure; the way man and woman were initially designed to be until we started messing it up with our foods, pollutions and sloth."

"So, what are you saying?" I asked.

"You are a human being," Eve replied.

I stood there a little confused; being human was a big blow to my ego. They essentially were telling me that I was like a child who was naturally born with steroids in his system, only, in my case, the steroids were made from other animal DNA. I was born to believe that I was a god and now I was being told that I was nothing, but a trans-human. The thought almost made me vomit.

"Enough chit-chat. Let's eat," Kozlov said.

I didn't say a word through dinner, while the professor talked about anything that came into his head.

Eve's gaze toward me had changed from animosity to compassion. As much as I couldn't stand the professor, I admired him. I realized that there were two reasons he made Eve rescue me after she tried to kill me. The first was that he didn't want my blood on her hands. He wanted her to be innocent of death. The second was that he wasn't sure how long Eve and I would live before we met our natural deaths. He believed that we could live up to 200 years, so he was hoping that we would be friends so that Eve would not be alone. Even still, the professor was a heartless, self-centered Russian, who had successfully demolished my pride and didn't even have the decency to notice.

"To bed we go, Adam. You can sleep here and we will talk more tomorrow," The professor said after dinner.

I looked at the man, this time genuinely mad that he couldn't respect my moment. He was acting as though he had told me that my shoes were blue. He kissed Eve on the cheek again, "Goodnight, my darling."

"Goodnight, father," she said warmly as her eyes remained on me, completely lacking aggression. When her father closed the door to his room, she asked, "Are you okay?" This question was the kindest thing I had ever heard come from her mouth. It was almost as though she understood my dilemma. She probably did as she could read my thoughts as I could read hers.

There was something overwhelming about the realization that I wasn't superman and her kindness toward me. For the first time since I could walk, tears began dripping from my eyes.

Shocked and embarrassed, I said, "What the hell is happening to me?" I tried to wipe away the tears, but they just kept streaming down my face.

"There is no shame in a few tears. They happen to everyone," she said.

"But not to me!" I screamed.

"You are me," she said gently and, with those words, I knew for sure that I was forever bonded to her.

"Why do you like them so much?" I asked.

"Them..." she let the word simmer, "for the same reasons you hate them."

"They are selfish," I coughed out the words.

"Some are selfless."

"They always want more than they already have."

"That's what allows them to survive."

"Survival," I guffawed.

She walked to the door. "True, the majority of them are selfish. They are quick to differentiate themselves from others based on race, religion or borders, but a few of them are so purely good that they make up for all of the negativity of the majority of the population." She opened the door and gestured for me to walk with her outside.

I walked with her down a hiking trail into the woods. We stepped on dead branches. The animals were hidden and quiet as we walked together into the night.

"What I love about people are the things they can do that you and I can't do. They are capable of art and creation. You and I can recite the 32 crystal class system, but we can't sing a note. We can replicate a painting, but we can't create our own, at least one that we will like," she said as she gracefully walked in front of me.

"You are right. I hate them for that, but can a human see another human and know everything about them? How they feel? What they love? What they need… the way you and I in our few moments of time together have been able to do? I can tell you the future that you and I will have, if you let it occur, and the divine thing about it is, unlike a human, you will know that it's the truth."

"There you go again with 'the humans'…" she said as she stopped by a tree and leaned her back on it. "You are human. You need to tattoo that onto your reality."

"You are deflecting my point."

"Maybe I am."

"It's not just about you and me; it's the perfection of this bond. I have never been so sure of myself that you and I are our futures. Do you feel differently?"

She squatted down, sitting on dead leaves. "There was a jujitsu school that I walked into once. In it, there was a black belt. Three men who had won world competitions had flew all the way from Brazil to train with this man. I was awed by the humility and respect that they had for him and the sport. For these three men to put their lives on hold to learn martial arts from someone better, humbled me. So, I joined the school to understand. I was stronger and faster than all of them, but I dampened my strengths to a minimum in order to learn and I learned and I understood."

"Your point is that I lack that humility."

"Yes. So, you and I are not as alike as you may think."

"Do you doubt my feelings?"

"No, not at all, but is that enough? I am still a child."

"You are 16 going on to a 100. You are more mature than the man you call father."

She continued talking as though I had said nothing. "And no matter how much you feel like a god because the people around you are weaker than you, there is still so much you need to learn."

"I don't understand what you are getting at," I said, confused.

She looked up into the sky at the stars shining brightly above the tree branches. Then, she closed her eyes and reached up as though she could touch them. "I love original music, not the recycled stuff, but music that is original. The beauty of a musical composition, the four movements of a symphony, the ability of a soulful voice to entice you or the unison of a choir."

"You think that you are better than me," I said the words much calmer than I wanted it voiced out.

"Why would you say that?" she asked, still looking up, but with her eyes closed, her fingers gently caressing the bark of the tree she was leaning on.

"You know that I am unable to understand music or art."

She looked at me, eyes wide open, "Really!?" She dug her hands into her afro hair. "Why would you think I knew that?"

"We are in each other's heads," I replied.

"Well, I didn't know that, so your theory is a little flawed."

"You think you are smarter than me," I said, getting peeved. I stood between her and a tree that had a two foot diameter.

"Does it matter?" she asked.

"Don't patronize me," I said, spitting out the words. "Let's see how smart you are. The Oxford

Electric Bell or Clarendon Dry Pile is an experimental electric bell that was set up when?"

She looked at me as though I was crazy, "Really? You want to do this."

"You don't know the answer."

"You said our brains are locked. Why don't you look into my mind and see whether I know the answer," she said sarcastically, dusting dirt off of her.

"I can't read anything."

"Exactly. You are only able to read my mind when I want you to."

I gave her a wicked smile. "So, that's a brilliant way of ducking the answer."

She looked back at me; the angry stare had returned. "Alright then, let's do this. The Clarendon Dry Pile was set up 1840. My turn. What happened to the wheel immediately after it was invented?"

I tapped my fingers on my forehead and began playing with answers in my head. I chose to talk out loud, so she could respect my train of thought. "It's not known who created the wheel, but it was invented in the late Neolithic period. When you say 'wheel,' are you referring to the wooden wheel?"

She looked at me with a bored expression. "When I say wheel, I mean wheel. No specifics."

It was pointless. I didn't know the answer and I was almost sure that she didn't, "I don't know."

"It caused a revolution," she replied with a smirk on her face.

"That wasn't funny. I am seriously trying to find myself by understanding you."

"Okay, a serious one," she said, as she tried to keep a straight face. "How many months in the year have 28 days?"

I knew it was another trick question, but I didn't care. "One."

"Wrong, all of the months have at least 28 days."

I smiled, "Semantics."

"Do I detect a smile in your physiognomy, sir?" she said with a cute, mocking expression.

I kept on smiling. I couldn't help it, I liked her. A sudden silence enveloped us. Then, I said, "We would need to leave?"

"Why?"

"The people who sent me here know where you are and they really want the professor. It's been a few hours. I don't think they will hone in on this place for the next 24 hours, but we still need to leave this-"

"We don't need to do anything," she responded adamantly. "I am tired of running and father is, too. All our lives we have run from continent to continent, country to country, town to town, village to village. We aren't running anymore."

"You have to believe me; you are dealing with a dangerous man."

"General Coriolanus Cole," she said. You could tell that she enjoyed the shock on my face. "I'm ready. Let the brunt of the military come. We are not running anymore."

"If not for yourself, then do it for the professor. We will put him somewhere safe and then we will run away from this humanity," I said.

"You are asking me to run away with you."

I dropped to my knee and held her hand, "I am begging you to run away with me. We will be happy. We will go somewhere we can be ourselves. We will have to hide who we are, for now until it's our time to take over this planet."

"And breed a better generation," she said in a sarcastic tone.

I let go of her hand and got back to my feet, a rush of anger swelling in me. "You are rejecting me."

"I am 16-years-old. I am a child still naïve to the world."

"You are lying to yourself. You are not a child. You are goddess living in the midst of degenerate mortals. You are staying because of the professor."

"Maybe, he needs me more than you."

"He is a grown man!" I screamed.

"He has been my mother and father for 16 years. When weak or strong, he has been my anchor. Now, some power hungry bastards are after him and you want me to leave him because you stumbled into our house six months ago to kidnap my father."

"Six months," I said confused. "I came here hours ago."

"No, you were in the cocoon for six months."

I put my hand to my head, confused. I looked crazily around the place as though I was in the twilight zone.

"After you entered the cocoon state, I expected the rest of your team to come banging on our door. I begged father to leave, but he made us stay because he wanted to watch over you."

I squatted down and banged my fingers to my head. "But why haven't they come?"

"Probably because of the General has been busy with the scandal that happened on the day you arrived. A whistleblower took a video of Ahmed Al-Harazi getting beaten in a military black site by a female soldier. Now, everyone is demanding General Coriolanus Cole identifies the soldier."

"Darshak," I said and jumped to my feet. I took a step away and then stepped back to her and stretched out my hand. "Come with me. We have a chance to create a symphony. I will call it Eve's Symphony or anything you want. It will touch our souls. It will outlive our mortality. It will forever remember our existence. It will grow the seed of perfection in this cursed planet."

"A child is not a symphony."

"Says who? Our children will be perfect. Please come with me."

She took my hand, walked close to me and then gently held me in her embrace. Then, she gently pulled my head down and kissed my forehead, "I'm sorry, Adam."

I looked her dead in the eye. "When next we meet, we meet as enemies and I will have to kill you."

"I'm used to meeting you that way. Goodbye, Adam."

"Goodnight, Eve." I said and then left, knowing that I would have to return to kill her.

General Coriolanus Cole

A man by the name of Jeremy Wong, who was supposed to be a soldier, was at our black site in Mexico to collect data for the Army Chief of Staff, General Lance Shockley. How he got the video of the T-soldier torturing Ahmed Al-Harazi is still a mystery to me. Everyone wanted results; they had turned a blind eye to how the results were gotten until some 40-year-old punk decided to load a video onto the internet. Suddenly, everyone had a bug in their underwear. Even the president was sweating blood; I literally had to hear his scrawny voice every other week. The man was controlled by polling sites, I was grateful that I didn't vote for him and, with the re-election coming up, he was becoming a drama queen.

After the soldiers volunteered for the restart program and their sexes changed, we didn't put their information into our database. Everything physical about the T-soldiers changed, including their fingerprints. Their DNA was the only thing that could connect them to their old selves. I had to admit that the T Soldiers made me proud. They had done more for their country than all of the soldiers who had ever served under me. They were precise and they observed the ultimate military law: come back with a successful mission or die trying.

Now, one of my soldiers, one of my comrades, was caught on tape because some hippie soldier didn't like the rules of war. It was all my fault. I expected General Shockley to have a true soldier working in his nest and not a stupid liberal. Now, it was my turn to face the hatchet of the media whores. The media didn't hesitate to create Armageddon out of the situation. They claimed a woman was used to humiliate Ahmed Al-Harazi because he was a Muslim man. They refused to believe that he was interrogated by the best soldier directly under my command. After Hosie died, Bubba was in charge. She, formerly a he, turned out to be a mighty fine soldier. It brought tears to my eyes to watch my T-soldiers operate. The beauty of a black site is that the people there can easily disappear, especially if their fingerprints and identities aren't in our system. The dilemma POTUS, his cabinet and the media were having was that they couldn't identify the soldier on the video and they knew that only I could.

The disgusting part in all of this fiasco was that they began treating Ahmed Al-Harazi as a war veteran; the man had successfully architected the deaths of 22 American soldiers and over a hundred foreign women and children. Keeping him alive had been my fault. We had drained him of all of the resources that he could provide and should have killed him.

I was facing the Senate Armed Service Committee the next day. Shockley summoned me to an empty warehouse in an abandoned army barracks in Virginia. The man was getting paranoid after the video leakage. I met him in the warehouse along with the Secretary of Defense, Adam O'Neill. Shockley was 57–years-old and was dressed sharply in his Army attire. His 5 foot 10 inch structure fit solidly in his uniform, but his askew hair gave his instability away. He had a full set of brown hair with tresses flowing over his forehead. His eyes were heavy, as though he hadn't slept in days. O'Neill looked relaxed. He had on a blue suit, white shirt and blue tie. He was balding in the center of his red hair and seemed tanned as though he had been under the sun for a while. He was 5 foot 6 inches and, at first glance, might seem the type you could trample on, but, I knew the man, he was a hard man.

"Secretary O'Neill, I didn't expect to see you," I said.

"Desperate times require desperate measures," he replied with a curt smile.

"We need her name Coriolanus," Shockley ordered, his words oozing desperation.

"I already told you. I ordered the command. The buck stops with me," I said.

"No, it doesn't Coriolanus. It ends with POTUS! The President of the United States," O'Neill said softly with a tone that grounded us all in his authority. He put his hands behind his back and looked around the empty warehouse as though he was thinking of building offices in the space. "I admire your loyalty to this soldier, but there are rules to the game and she got caught."

"Seven," I said.

"Seven what!?" Shockley coughed out the response, unable to contain his anger.

"Seven terrorist attacks were stopped by the actions of that soldier in the video. Some of those attacks were geared toward American women and children. Did she get even a congratulatory call from POTUS when that happened? No. Now, because some liberal nut who claims to be a soldier uploads a video on some site, she is an enemy of the state."

"Is she your lover?" O'Neill asked suspiciously.

"No, she is my soldier, a soldier under my command, a soldier who has done more for this country than even I have," I replied.

"You see what I have to deal with," Shockley said to O'Neill, pointing at me as though I was not there.

"Coriolanus, I need you to understand what you are doing and saying. This is an all or nothing situation. We need the name," O'Neill said, softly.

"We are a democracy, for goodness sake!" Shockley yelled. "We serve at the pleasure of the president, who, in turn, is voted in and out based on what the people want. Now, the people want the soldier who committed the crime."

"Everyone keeps calling it torture. It was a fair fight between two people who carry weapons for their causes," I said, trying to enlighten them.

"It is not a fair fight if everyone outside the walls around you is your enemy," O'Neill said.

"It's not torture in my book," I said, standing my ground.

"When you torment a man or woman to get them to say or do what you want, then that is torture, even if you aren't water boarding them or using a weapon. It is torture even if it's a woman beating a man," O'Neill said, looking at me as though I had just killed a man.

"As I've said a million times before, it was my call and I will take responsibility for my actions," I said as I involuntarily stood at attention.

"Coriolanus...," O'Neill said my name as though I was his lover. "Coriolanus, Coriolanus, Coriolanus... What happens to our boys if they get captured? If we let this soldier get away, then we let the world know that it is okay to torture an American soldier if they think they are in the right."

"If the American soldier is a terrorist, then he deserves what's coming to him," I replied.

"One man's terrorist is another man's freedom fighter," O'Neill said as he took a deep breath. "The whole world understands that you and only you can help identify this soldier. The majority of the army corp. is on your side for this and we-"

"By we, you mean POTUS," I interjected.

"Yes, by we, I mean the President of the United States. We think it will lead to an unfortunate avalanche of events if you get fired, especially with your cult status. So, since you will still not give us her name, there is only one option left." He looked around again; making sure that no one was listening in this isolated warehouse. He took out a sheet of paper and wrote on it before handing it to me.

The note said, "Lie under oath tomorrow. Tell them that you do not know who the woman is."

I looked up at them and said, "I serve at the pleasure of the president. Is this... what he wants?"

"Can I have that back?" O'Neill asked. I handed him the note and he tore it into tiny pieces and put it into his breast pocket. "Everything I say or do is what he wants."

"Nobody will believe it," I said.

"It's not about belief. It's about perception and humility," O'Neill continued. "In your head its honor; in ours, its defiance. If you humble yourself, take your beating from those corrupt senators and congressman, show the press that, indeed, you feel there was something wrong with the torture, then you will put us in a better place than we are in right now."

I massaged my head with my fingers, "Everything I've done, I did for my country and I will do it again in a heartbeat."

"Yada yada yada, great, you're a patriot. Are we on the same page?" Shockley asked impatiently.

"Think of your wife, your boys...the army," O'Neill said, the last words slithering into my head smoothly.

"Yes," I said the words and I felt this weight press against me, pulling me down to the Earth. The last time I had this feeling, it was in the Mona Islands, watching my beautiful, loyal soldiers disappear into smoke because of another snitch. This time, I was going to protect my soldiers at the expense of any and everything I loved. All of these years I had sacrificed for my country and I had gotten nothing in return, just promotions that had put me in more compromising positions.

O'Neill put his hand on my shoulder and said, "This way, everyone hurts equally." Then, he walked away, followed by Shockley, who didn't bother to look my way as they left me alone in the warehouse.

***

At the Senate Armed Services Committee, I sat on the left of O'Neill. On his right was Shockley, dressed in full regalia like myself and showing all of his medals for the world to see. In front of and above us, purposely to give them some false sense of superiority, were 34 senators, who couldn't miss an opportunity to show themselves on every news channel other than the ever present C-SPAN. The reporters were doing what they did best, hissing around like the brood of vipers they were. The audience was seated behind us. Behind them, I could hear protesters, but I wasn't bothered by them as they were insignificant pawns.

"Traitor! Traitor!" The crowds screamed at me. Another group sang in chorus, "Lock Coriolanus in an anus! Lock Coriolanus in an anus!" One or two were bold enough to take the racket to the next level, "Execute Coriolanus."

I don't know why, but just the sound of these hippies screaming for justice in the platform of peace for which I and my brothers-in-arms fought and bled made me smirk. The senator from Wisconsin, Marianne Andrews, a fragile looking 61-year-old woman with thick bifocals, seemed disgusted by the smirk.

The chairman of the committee was the senior senator from Virginia, Bob Devlin, a balding six foot three inch, loquacious, white 61-year-old. He finished talking about the magnitude of what happened as though we had invaded a country and then the 78-year-old senator from West Virginia, Jack Thomas, took over. He talked about the army as though he knew true honor; it was an open secret that, in Vietnam, he shot himself in the foot to get away.

"I'll ask our witnesses to rise," Devlin said in his baritone voice. We all stood up. "Do each of you solemnly swear that the testimony that you are about to give to the Committee on the Armed Services of the United States will be the truth, the whole truth and nothing but the truth, so help you God?"

"I do," all three of us answered congruously and sat down.

Devlin began rambling about the security of the country and all of the events that he believed the leaked video could unleash. After all his wasted words he said, "The complete statements of the witnesses will be placed into the record. Yesterday, the committee received opening remarks from the secretary, followed by the chairman of the joint chiefs. I'm not certain if others desire some recognition for the opening remarks. If so, indicate to the chair, and then we'll go into a 5-minute round of questions by each member."

Everyone turned their heads toward me. I said, "At this point, no." Both O'Neill and Shockley had explicitly begged or, maybe, warned me, I am not sure anymore which it was, not to give any opening remarks. They didn't trust the words that would come out of my mouth and I didn't blame them.

"Then, we'll proceed with the questions," Devlin said. "It's obvious that the gregarious nature of this case as it unfolds, especially its effect on our relationship with other nations, our foreign policy, is disastrous to our image. So, I ask you, what is that impact, as best you can assess it today?"

O'Neill sighed, a measured attempt to show the gravity of the situation. "I will let history give a better certainty of the end results of the video, but our allies and the world know that this rogue soldier doesn't represent the United States Army and that this individual will be found and persecuted to the full extent of the law."

"Thank you, sir," Devlin said.

"Mr. Chairman, if I could just add," beads of sweat had already started gathering on Shockley's forehead, "Just last week, I returned from a NATO military committee meeting and had the chance to talk to several of our allies in the fight against terrorism. Their support for our common goal hasn't faltered."

"That is good to know," Devlin responded. "My next question is to you General Shockley. What is your opinion of Captain Jeremy Wong? Is he a hero, terrorist, whistleblower or good soldier?"

Pockets of screams of "Hero!" came from behind me. I didn't bother to look at the parasites; what did they know about the code of war.

"I believe that Jeremy Wong is a hero and good soldier. I'm proud to say that he remains under my service due to his exemplary work." The crowd behind me went into a spontaneous applause.

"My time has expired. Senator Thomas?"

"Thank you, Mr. Chairman," the older, veteran senator said as he arranged several sheets of paper in front of him. Then, he looked me dead in the eye, soldier to soldier and asked, "General Coriolanus Cole, I would like to ask you the same question. Do you think Captain Jeremy Wong is a hero?"

I dreaded this question. The room fell so silent that the camera flashes flickering across the room sounded like thunderstorms. I thought Senator Thomas, as a veteran, would have been my ally on the committee, but, by throwing this question to me, it seemed that wasn't the case.

"I..." I cleared my throat. O'Neill and Shockley kept looking straight ahead as though I wasn't there.

"I.... what?" Thomas asked impatiently. Every one of those bloody civilians started laughing at me.

I sucked it up. I was doing this for the army. "I think he is a civilian hero."

The murmurs in the room grew loud.

"A civilian hero? What does that mean?"

"He means the people's hero," O'Neill jumped in.

"Secretary O'Neill, you are not new to how this committee works. You answer only those questions addressed to you," Devlin cut in.

"Sorry, Mr. Chairman," O'Neill replied, leaning back into his chair.

"He is the people's hero," I said into the microphone.

"And to the army? Is he a hero for showing the atrocities committed by our soldiers?" the hard core conservative was getting liberal on me. The man must have hated me more than his principles.

I waited for a moment and then leaned into the microphone, "Was that a question or a statement?" There were two giggles behind me.

"This is not a joke," Thomas said. "The lives of our boys fighting for this great country are in danger because of the atrocities committed on the tape."

"Thank you, Senator," Devlin said.

"My time is up," the senator said with a wide grin, the stupid old coward and shameful excuse for a soldier had succeeded in vexing me more than I expected of any senator.

"Senator Andrews," Devlin said.

"Thank you. General Shockley," she said as she took of her glasses and gently placed them on some papers on the table in front of her. "I sit here with a huge sense of sorrow at the state of affairs of soldiers like this, even if they are few. With such a situation, how can we trust that this was a onetime occurrence and that there weren't any more soldiers involved with this type of behavior who didn't get caught?"

"As the chief of staff of the Army," Shockley said, "I am responsible for the training and equipping of our soldiers and developing our Army leaders into the giants they will become. I am also responsible for providing ready and relevant land power capabilities to the combatant commanders and the joint team. Although not in the operational chain of command, I am responsible for our soldiers' training and readiness. Therefore, it is very personal to me when any of my soldiers fail to meet the exemplary standards we expect of them. To your question, this is just one individual, who doesn't represent my men. This behavior has no place in the character of our soldiers."

O'Neill kept nodding his head in agreement as Shockley spoke. I just looked straight ahead, with my head held high. That seemed to peeve the senators.

"General Shockley, this…black site that Ahmed Al-Harazi was beaten up at, why aren't we aware of this location?" Andrews asked.

"I too wasn't aware of this location. My aide, Captain Wong, was directed to meet with General Cole at a specified location regarding the transportation of Ahmed Al-Harazi and he was rerouted to this location." Shockley throwing me under the bus didn't just take me by surprise, but even O'Neill was shocked by the blatant lie. They all knew why we couldn't take Ahmed Al-Harazi directly from Yemen to the United States as, once in America, every terrorist had access to get the best lawyer's money can buy.

"So, I direct the question to General Coriolanus Cole," she said my full name sarcastically. "Why wasn't anyone informed of this black site?"

"It wasn't a black site, ma'am," I responded.

"Then what was it?" she asked impatiently.

"A transit point," I said and the crowd, who was venomously against me, began to titter.

"This is not a joke, general!" her voice screeched through the microphone.

"I'm not laughing, ma'am," I answered straight-faced.

"Traitor! Traitor!" The chant started with one person behind me and then the crowd followed. I watched these people, who lived under the protection that I provided them, call me a traitor and my face radiated pure rage.

"This... disgrace of a soldier," Andrews continued, "Who is she? Where is she? And why hasn't anyone got any information on her?"

She directed the question at all three of us, but O'Neill and Shockley just turned their heads toward me, making it vividly clear who was to take the fall. The word 'traitor' kept ringing in my head; the senators and reporters, every one of them, wanted me to hang, but not hang alone.

The room went dead silent as I spoke, "Archaeologists and ancient texts believe that shaking hands only goes back to the 5th century during ancient Greece, but it goes further back. With the norms of our lazy society, we believe in our liberal views of everything, including the handshake. The handshake was, and is, still used to know the difference between friend and foe. The more clandestine the handshake, the more selective the group."

"Thank you for the education," she said sarcastically. "Now, please, would you answer my question before my time runs out?" The crowd burst out, laughing at me. Some of the senators snickered.

I waited for the laughter to die down to murmurs and then I said, "I have served this country for 42 years." The room went dead silent. "Now, you all think I am is a joke."

"That was not my intention," Andrew's said, quickly seeing a backlash coming her way.

I ignored her and continued, "Three tours in Vietnam, Laos 1974 military support, 1975 evacuation from Cambodia, Operation Eagle Pull, Korea 1976, Zaire 1978, 1983 Operation Urgent Fury, 1987 Operation Earnest Will, 1988 Operation Golden Pheasant, 1989 Panama, Operation Just Cause, 1990 Operation Desert Shield, 1991 Operation Desert Storm, 1992 Operation Restore Hope, 1994 Operation Uphold Democracy-"

Thomas cut in, "You are not the only one who has served in this room. Answer the senator's question." The room broke out into a loud applause and the senator turned to the chairman, "Forgive me, Mr. Chairman." Devlin nodded his head in appreciation.

When the applause died down, I continued as though the senator hadn't interrupted me. "As I said, those are just a few of the wars my name is stamped on. There are many, many things that I have done and bled for my country that you will never know about. These people behind me who refer to me as a traitor and you, the people who represent them, sit in your succulent chairs and don't have the common decency to correct them. I am of the mind that you all speak in unison." O'Neill's eyes zoned in on me, directly warning me without words. "Now to your questions. Who is she? She is the perfect soldier, loyal to the core, who has done more for this country than all of you senators sitting there, including that coward who shot himself in the foot to escape Vietnam instead of watching his brothers' backs." I paused and looked at Senator Thomas, waiting for him to reply to my comment. "Where is she? That is none of your business. Why hasn't anyone got any information on her? Because I knew that one day people like you, who are the first to scream when a terrorist attacks, will also scream about how we keep the terrorist's out when the world finds out." O'Neill put his hand on his head in frustration; Shockley kept his face straight ahead as though I was invisible. The senators watched me in shock, the reporters were going crazy around me, jockeying for the best shots of me. The crowd behind me had fallen silent. Nobody wanted to put their faces on the line, when the lion was hungry for prey. "There have been 29 terrorists attack averted from the information that this soldier, whom the media calls Soldier Red, has gotten from the terrorist Ahmed Al-Harazi. And I emphasize, the *terrorist* Ahmed Al-Harazi. When the Boston bombers attacked, America stopped for the day, imagine that feeling happening 18 times in our country and another 11 times in the different parts of the world that he planned to attack. As for Captain Wong, he is a civilian hero, but a military traitor. Any man who would throw a fellow soldier, a brother who would take a bullet for him, under the bus is worth less than the dirt under my feet. So, let me state this unequivocally, I will never give up the identity or location of the 'hero' and I emphasize *hero* named Soldier Red. I will be handing in my resignation and I am ready for whatever punishment my actions cause me." I stood and walked out of the room. No one attempted to stop me. They just parted from me as though I was a virus.

Soldier Red

Three teardrops fell from my eyes as I watched my general, live on TV. I wasn't hiding. It's funny, when a female soldier puts on a dress, it's almost as though she changed from Batman to Bruce Wayne. I knew that I had to change my hair color from red, but the whole Soldier Red thing was really beginning to grow on me. Apart from that, nearly every woman was suddenly cutting her hair short and dyeing it red because of the notoriety of the videos. The full video captured everything that happened that day. Ahmed Al-Harazi threw the first punch, which I let him do. After that, I gave him a humiliating beat down and the man sang like a canary.

The first time I joined the army, all I wanted to do was kill a man, but, contrary to the movies, that opportunity didn't come easily. I got into a fight with a weasel and I almost killed him. They were about to kick me out of the army with a dishonorable discharge and all I had to go back to was an unfaithful girlfriend who claimed I was the father of her baby. So, when they asked for volunteers for a secret program, I was like "hell yes." The beauty of it all was that, after the experiment, I was legally dead. I didn't exist. I didn't have much to go back to in Mississippi, so it was perfect for me. Things changed when they did their experiment on me. I became faster, stronger, smarter. Things that took months to figure out, took me minutes. My target shooting became perfect. The only problem was that my body started to change. I suddenly began growing breasts, my voice became higher, my Adam's apple disappeared, my penis began to shrink and, the next thing I knew, I had a vagina. The odd part about it all was that somehow my mind was more comfortable as a woman. I wasn't even attracted to women anymore. It was literally a life changing experience.

Anyway, after the hybrid human or whatever that thing they called Adam got Ahmed Al-Harazi, it was my job to get as much information from him as possible before handing him down. So, I did my duty. Unfortunately, it was filmed by another soldier. How he got the video is a mystery to me. When the video leaked, I begged my general to let me surrender, but he let me know that it wasn't only about me but the other 21 T-soldiers like me, whose identities might be forced to go public if I surrendered. Only three people had known our past identities. The first died of a heart attack. The second died while skydiving. The only living person was General Coriolanus Cole: my general.

I was the captain and commanding officer of the 21 T-soldiers. I stood in the abandoned, underground military bunker in the Sonoran Desert in Arizona. It was 30 feet underground and 29 steps descending down into it. A gray steel door closed us off from the world. It was 10 feet high and 12 feet wide. The entrance was designed to withstand a nuclear explosion. It had enough room to house 1,100 people and was built to match the specs of the Greenbrier bunker: 112,000 square feet on two subterranean levels, with the de-contamination showers; 433 feet of long, gray tunnel that lead to the bunker after walking past the steel door; 153 rooms; 18 dormitories; a 12-bed hospital; a power plant; a TV studio and separate chambers for the House and the Senate members in case of a nuclear Armageddon. It was a secret bunker for members of congress that was never disclosed publicly and very few members of the military were aware of it. It was built during President Eisenhower's time in office.

I walked between the soldiers who were lined up at attention, facing each other. They all had on camouflage pants and black t-shirts. Every one of the soldiers had their hair cut short. They were of all races and had come to love their female bodies as I had, so I presumed that the experiment pushed our minds to work that way.

I looked every one of them in the eye and they all looked back at me without flinching, "Gear up. The party is about to begin."

General Coriolanus Cole

It had been three days since the senate committee meeting. I tried to get access to the president to give him my resignation, but I wasn't allowed anywhere near him, so I decided to meet with the Secretary of Defense, who was conveniently away when I asked to make an appointment. I understood their furtive attempt to use me as the guinea pig and I was okay with it, but the sudden ignorance and deliberate attempts to prevent me from accepting my fate was downright unprofessional. On the third day, out of the blue, O'Neill asked me to come over to his office. The shocking thing about the appointment is that he didn't keep me waiting, which made me wonder what type of kryptonite they had planned.

When I walked into his office, he stood against the outside of his desk, waiting for me. I had barely taken three steps when he walked toward me and shook my hand.

"Coriolanus," he said.

"Secretary O'Neill," I responded, my resignation letter in hand.

He led me to a brown sofa beside the door. He had left the office almost exactly the way his predecessor had, except that he added the new president's picture and added a stand up desk. I was dressed in uniform and he had on a navy blue suit. When we got to the sofa, he chose to stand by the sofa. He deliberately wanted me standing.

"So, what can I do for you?" he asked as though oblivious to everything going on.

"I am having a problem finding anyone to hand my resignation to."

"No, Coriolanus, we won't accept your resignation," O'Neill said taking a seat. At that point, I suddenly felt fulfilled that they appreciated my years of service and respected my loyalty to my country and my men, enough to keep me on after those stupid politicians attempted to soil my name.

"I see," I said as signs of a gratified smile escaped the sides of my lips. The army was my life and I was proud that the people's president had recognized that. "So, what are my orders?" I asked, standing proud.

"You have none Coriolanus. You are fired. This is straight from POTUS." O'Neill did not lose eye contact with me as he spoke.

I felt my spirit leave my body as shock overtook me. It took me a moment to understand what was going on. "I didn't deserve the courtesy to be told by the president in person?"

"That's the least of your problems," he said matter-of-factly, "Charges will be brought against you and you will need to find yourself a damn good attorney."

I looked at this little man, who armed with enormous power, was acting as the weapon of my destruction. He didn't, for one second, realize that, in the last few seconds, he took away the most important thing in my life and, even worse than my resignation, let me know that I was on the verge of getting dishonorably discharged for doing my job. Not once did this little man contemplate that I could grab his skull and smash it into the wall.

"Thank you for your time," I said. We shook hands again.

"By the way, a little heads up," he said, holding my hand and looking me dead in the eye. "The attorney general is keen on this going to trial in civilian court with jurors and not the military court, so you shouldn't narrow your options."

A final blow to my ego. They knew my peers had nothing, but respect for my sacrifices and that civilians were just parasites who believed everything they watched on TV. No other words were shared, just a hard silence. He left me standing by myself as he returned to his desk. I walked to the door and then stopped to look back at him, but he had already gone back to work. I walked out of his office with no second thoughts as to what had to be done. I was prepared.

Adam

The problem with security is that everyone puts all of their sensors above the ground. No one ever thinks that the culprit could come from underground. General Coriolanus Cole's home was isolated in Virginia. His house was built on a 1.55 acre, two story brick farmhouse built in 1810, but renovated inside and out. It had many mature trees around it, extensive landscaping and an in-ground pool. The beams framing the doorway and kitchen were originally floor joists. The house had radiant heated floors and many windows overlooking the original smokehouse. A spiraling staircase led to the three bedrooms upstairs, all of which had oak doors. The master bedroom had an extensive master bath with a glass block shower and large tub.

He was soaking into the bathtub when I walked in; his eyes were closed as Luciano Pavarotti belted Ave Maria from his stereo speakers.

"Have they fired you?" I asked him.

"They did one better. They are going to arrest me and drag me through civilian court," he said, finally looking at me.

"You can't blame them with the elections coming up. What other way is there to get the votes than to publicly humiliate the most hated American?"

He smiled and said, "I have a job for you." He stood and grabbed his towel, drying the soapy lather off his body.

"Well, about that. You see since you got fired, it means that you don't represent the United States of America anymore, so anything I do for you would be as a vigilante," I said as I walked with him into the bedroom. He began putting on his military uniform. "It's 8:30 at night. Please don't tell me that you sleep in your uniform."

"Sorry, I forgot to mention that, at 9, they are coming to arrest me. They wanted it at night, so that the press wouldn't make a spectacle," he said as he tied the shoelaces of his polished shoes.

"How considerate."

"Well, if you are not going to help me, then why are you here?" he asked.

I looked around. "Where are your wife and sons?"

"They were not aware that I got fired. My wife is at her sister's house and my sons are on duty. Why are you here?"

"Darshak."

The general smiled, "I have never been sure where your passions lie...if it was the ability to cause destruction in the name of good or whether Darshak was your toy."

"You realize that I will have to torture you to get Darshak's location?"

"I have been tortured before," he said with a smirk on his face.

"But, not by me."

"You want to know the secret about being tortured.... everyone talks, some sooner, some later, but everyone talks."

"I'm glad you see the future."

"I'm sorry that I gave you the wrong impression. It's like this, Adam, every single human being who knows what you look like or what you are capable of are..." Cole paused to look at his watch. "dead by accidental causes. They fell down a staircase, had a heart attack and all that ordinary stuff, nothing flashy. There are only four people left alive who know about you. Besides me, there is Dr. Darshak Khurana, Professor Kozlov and the girl. Forgive me, I forgot about Dakota Knox. She's nowhere to be found, but, when we find her, we will kill her. Now, I need you to understand this, everyone left alive is alive because I want them alive."

"Are you threatening me?"

"No, I am telling you. I am the only link to you existing in the manner that you want. Without me, you are nothing, but an illegal alien."

"What's the job?" I asked, resigned.

He looked around his room. He was almost sure his house was bugged. He raised his index finger to the ceiling and said, "I want you to introduce Bubba to God."

How I knew what he meant scared me more than the request itself, "That's impossible."

"Impossible for the ordinary," he said with a smile. "Will you make the introduction?"

"It's impossible."

"Are you afraid of dying or afraid of failing?" he asked, smiling. I didn't know how to respond and he looked at me with shame. He walked over to his desk drawer, "What I always loved about you Adam is that you always understood me, regardless of how I chose to communicate with you. I doubt even the people listening in on this conversation have any idea of what I just asked of you." He opened a drawer full of well-ironed handkerchiefs; he picked one up and put it in his breast pocket. "You're probably the greatest existence on this planet, but what makes you inferior to the T-soldiers is that they do not have any fear. They are loyal to the bone and failure for them is not an option."

I turned toward him angrily. My quills tore out through my back and arms, tearing holes through my hooded shirt. I would have punched him, but he looked back at me with disappointment and, suddenly, my anger turned to shame at my weakness.

"Your weakness breaks my heart more than it can ever break yours," He said as his doorbell rang. He straightened his uniform and said, "It's time to face the dragon."

He walked passed me and down the spiraling stairs. When he opened the door, two Army men read him his rights and led him to the black SUV waiting outside. As I looked out the window, watching them take him away under the moonlight, I saw a T-soldier. She had high cheekbones with a reddish brown complexion and, unlike the other T-soldiers, she was beautiful. I was positive that she wasn't one of them; she didn't smell like them. She was two miles away, looking at me from the trees with her binoculars. She knew I was in the room and that I could see her. She smiled as she tapped on the transmitter on her chest, a gesture to let me know she was listening. She winked at me and jumped down from the tree. Then, she got into her jeep and drove off. I contemplated chasing after her, but I was emotionally exhausted by my sudden fear of death and failure, and of which seemed to be rooted in meeting the professor and that crazy Eve. Something about the meeting with Eve suddenly made my life necessary to me. I suddenly found it necessary to continuously exist, if possible, forever.

General Lance Shockley

I was lying in bed with my mistress, Charlene, in a five star hotel in my pajamas when the lights went out in the building. The room went pitch black. It was pointless waking Charlene as she was in a deep sleep. I walked blindly to the window to investigate what was going on. I opened the curtains and noticed that the lights were out down the entire block. The opening in the curtains let in a sliver of light that helped to illuminate the room a little bit. I headed toward the door, aided by the moonlight, when I felt a needle pierce my neck. I immediately lost consciousness.

When I woke up, I found myself on the floor with a dirty black sack on my head. My hands were tied behind my back. Then, someone cut the ropes from my hands and unmasked me. I found myself on a high school basketball court surrounded by four female soldiers. The women were all about 6 feet tall in great shape with short hair. They had protruding hips and shapely breasts. The only problem with their aesthetics was their faces; they were so hard that they were unappealing. One was Asian and three were white. The Asian soldier was the shortest. She had on black gloves and was closest to me. Tied to a chair under the basketball rim with his hands behind his back and mouth gagged was Jeremy Wong. He was wearing only his underwear, which was smirched by the blood that dripped from his face and body. The chair sat on 12 black trash bags.

The Asian soldier stood in front of me at attention, "Hello general. I am First Lieutenant Kwan, team leader. Sorry for the circumstances under which you were brought."

"How dare you, lieutenant? I will make sure you get court martialed for this," I yelled, angry at the disrespect from a common lieutenant, forgetting I was the prisoner.

"Court martialed by which army?" Kwan asked. I didn't understand what she meant. She looked at the three soldiers and they spread across the room, one went to the entrance door leading in and out of the court, the other marched up the stairs to the top of the audience benches and the last one stood by the exit door by the audience benches. "You know the army military rule on adultery, don't get caught," she replied.

"Lieutenant, you will remember who you are speaking to," I warned her.

"I had a bloody conversation with Jeremy Wong. He told me that you sent him to film the whole thing and, of course, I wouldn't expect a man of your military loyalty to be so unfaithful to the corp., so I beat him up some more. However, he made a good point. He wasn't there during the beat down; he only knew where it was taking place. So, all he did was put a satellite camera in the room. You were aware that the interrogation was taking place and all you had to do was record it when the sensors awoke on the camera."

"What are you accusing me off?"

"We are not accusing you of anything. We know the answer to the question we are asking. Look at Jeremy," Kwan pointed at my aide, bleeding and unconscious. "Does he look like a man with any lies left to give?"

"Are you going to kill him?"

"Yes," she answered matter-of-factly.

"And Charlene?" I asked, worried for my mistress. She was a good woman who knew how to make me love again, feel in a way that my wife felt was unnecessary.

"We are soldiers, not barbarians," she said. "She is still asleep in bed. The drug should wear off in 12 hours. She will wake up thinking that you left her to go home to your wife."

I sighed, "So what happens now?"

"You tell us why you snitched on us and we would also like to know your itinerary for the entire week."

"Snitched," I laughed when I heard the word used by this child. "And if I don't?"

"I will give you the same option that I gave to Jeremy, you walk passed me through the door and you are free," Kwan said with a straight face.

"And your weapons?" I asked, laughing at the proposal.

"No weapons," she replied.

"Four women without weapons against me...that seems fair," I said seriously. She seemed to think I was being sarcastic.

"The other soldiers have been ordered to stand down. The only person you have to pass is me," she said with her arms behind her back.

I laughed when she uttered those words. I was a battle-tested general. Me against the four women would have been an unfair fight against them. Against one, it wouldn't even be a fight.

"If you insist," I said. I quickly threw a jab and a cross; she remained in the same spot and dodged my punches. "Impressive reflexes," I said. She remained expressionless, looking at me as though I was a boring jester. I threw three punches and kicked at her. She dodged all of my attacks, only, this time, she moved her body sideways to avoid my kick toward her midsection. She kept within an arm's length of me, continuously staring at me as though I was a toddler screaming for a toy. I had run out of patience, so I rushed at her and attempted to tackle her. She jumped six feet over me and I fell to the floor, landing on my arms. I quickly turned toward her and got back to my feet.

"Permission to speak freely, general," she said with her arms still behind her back.

"You kidnapped me in the middle of the night and now you're asking my permission to speak?" I asked, frustrated, already losing my breath, my pajamas had ripped on the knees from my fall.

"I take it that I don't have your permission so I will align this conversation to the mission at hand. You have five minutes for this foreplay and, then, I will begin to inflict pain on you."

"Give me your best shot," I said, raising my fists in front of my face. I didn't see her punch coming, but it went between my hands and smashed into my face. It felt as though I had been hit by a refrigerator. The force flung me off my feet and I bashed into the benches. I blanked out for a moment. When I opened my eyes, my nose was broken, my face drenched in blood and my back was severely bruised where the bench broke my fall.

Kwan stood over me, no sign of glee on her face from my humiliation. "First question," she said, confident that I would answer. "Why?"

I looked at her in disbelief wondering whether any human could possess that amount of power and I decided that she could not be human. "What are you?" I asked.

She grabbed me by the neck and swung me over her head like a towel. Then, she bashed me against the basketball court. She stood over me, letting the moment drown in the pain. I couldn't feel parts of my body and the parts I could feel came with excruciating pain.

She didn't have to say another word; I started talking. "I needed a scandal like Abu Ghraib to make the president vulnerable in his party for someone to contest his spot in the election." So much for death before dishonor. I motioned away from her, aided by my shoulders, covering my bleeding face from any form of attack.

"Why?" she asked, her voice was high, but after the pain she had dished out to me, she sounded like a titan talking to an ant.

"If James Luger runs against him in the Democrat party, it will split the votes and give room that the Republican candidate can use to win," I spoke as loudly and as fast as I could. I didn't want to give her any reason to hit me again.

"Which Republican candidate?"

"Dakota Knox."

As soon as I said the name, she called for one of the other soldiers. When she got to her side, she whispered something in her ear and the soldier left the gym.

"What's in it for you?" she asked.

"Secretary of Defense," I said, spitting out the blood that had dripped into my mouth.

The soldier at the top of the staircase walked down to her and said, "The place is too bloody, we don't have time to clean it up."

"True," she said. Then, she pulled my SIG pro semi-automatic pistol from a black plastic bag. I always hid it under the seat of my car. I noticed that she was wearing gloves; she didn't want her fingerprints on the gun. I offered not an iota of resistance as she placed the gun in my weakened arms and pulled the trigger, killing Jeremy Wong. Even in my present state, I couldn't help, but admire her marksmanship, the bullet went straight into the middle of his head. She was setting me up; I knew it and I preferred that option to any form of beat down that she could easily deliver. She threw the gun close to Jeremy's dead body. Then, she lifted me up onto her shoulder as if I didn't weight anything before ordering the other soldiers to "Burn the place."

EVE

Why we aren't running is a little confusing to me. All of my life, it was all about "them." Father never told me who "them" was, but I knew it had to be something big, a group, a powerful group; however, I didn't think it was a secret organization in the United States army. When Adam arrived, it was our cue to run, but father used saving him as an excuse to stay and I obliged because, unknown to him, I knew we didn't have any more money. What nobody tells you in the movies is that it cost a lot of money to go on the run. I brought up the option of robbing a bank as a serious suggestion laced around a joke and father completely barked at the suggestion. Truth be told, we were happy. We owned the house and we had a large garden a few yards away with most of the food we needed. If we didn't go on the run, we had enough to live out the rest of our lives. I loved the place, so did father. Father especially loved the library that was 10 miles away; he seemed to have a voracious literary appetite for updated knowledge and our proximity from the town made internet connection difficult.

The oddest thing happened this time before father decided to go to the library, he said, "I have never told you, maybe because you have never asked, but you have always known and I chose to play ignorant about it. Your mother was… I loved your mother." I didn't know how to react to that. True, since the day I was born; I had never fit a mother in the puzzle of my life even though I knew one existed. He stood there for a long moment, expecting some response, but I had none to give. Maybe I should have asked who she was, what she was, but I just didn't feel it was necessary to care. He pulled me into his arms and kissed me on the forehead. Then, in his normal, genteel manner, he said, "Going to the library."

After he left, for an hour I rehearsed how to broach the topic of my mother, maybe he wanted me to ask where she was or how she was doing. I knew that I needed to ask because he wanted me to. I loved the man as much as any daughter loved a father. He was there for me in every type of weather, rain, sun or snow. He understood what I was way before I even began to understand what I was. He put me first before everything. I didn't understand how any daughter could repay that kind of love.

I was cleaning the house, when I felt it. I knew the feeling. I could sense the professor. The further away he was, the smaller the intensity of that sudden rush of blood in my heart. He was far away and in trouble. In that same moment, I heard a bang on the door.

A female voice said, "We would like to talk to you about your father? He is presently on a helicopter high in the sky so that you can't track him."

They were 10 people around the house. I could hear the clicking of their submachine guns, but no increased heartbeats, which meant that they didn't know what I was capable of or I didn't have an idea what I was about to face. Every person has a smell that, to me, differentiates them from every other animal, but these intruders had doused themselves with something that deflected their scent, which is why I couldn't smell them from further away. My presumption was simple, whoever did the talking was probably the person with the greatest knowledge of where my father was. I had on blue jeans and a black t-shirt on which were the words "When Gods Bleed" written in red. In my head, I seemed composed, but my body was telling me a different story, quills had spiked out of my back, legs and arms, tearing through my jeans and t-shirt. My father was everything to me; without him, there was no way I would exist. He lived for me and I lived for him. There were no negotiations necessary; they were all going to die.

I smashed through the back wall and grabbed one of the female soldiers who was carrying a M249 light machine gun. I broke her neck and arm, killing her instantly. As soon as the other soldiers saw me, they sprayed bullets in my direction. I used her dead body as shield and flung her at two of the other soldiers. The force knocked them off of their feet and the commotion caused the other soldiers to run to the back of the house. I leapt up into the air and landed on the roof, running to the front of the house. Only one soldier remained on that side of the building. The claws that grew out of my feet tore into her shoulder. She writhed in pain as she fell to her knees, but she didn't scream. She turned her mk48 toward me and, with a strength I had never seen in a normal human being, fired a shot before I broke her neck by forcefully kicking her head backward.

A howitzer of bullets followed as I moved at 78 miles an hour into the forest. Once into the forest, I climbed up a basswood tree and stood watching the remaining eight female soldiers. Seven of the soldiers entered the forest and I watched closely. I needed to make sure I knew which one was giving the orders. All of the soldiers were dressed in camouflage. They were carrying machine guns that would have been too heavy for a strong man to carry. They all had on helmets and were dressed for battle. They knew what they were coming up against. I saw their leader, how could I miss her, Soldier Red. She was the only one who stayed behind by the house, standing in the middle of the driveway. I saw the pride that the seven soldiers took as they walked into my forest, on my land, as though they were hunters and I was their prey. They split in two groups, each soldier walking 15 feet from the other.

On a normal day, I would have watched and toyed with them, but, now, the longer I waited, the worse my chances were for getting my father back. I landed on the shrubs softly, just as they passed under my tree. In the instant that it took one of the soldiers to look back at me, I punched my hand through her face, killing her. Another soldier fired at me, but I grabbed her gun and threw it like a like a spear through her gut, killing her instantly before she could fire another shot. I used the second soldier as a shield, as the fourth soldier shot. Then, I flung the dead soldier at her. The weight bashed the two of them into the tree. I punched through the third soldier's back and through the fourth soldier's chest until I hit the tree. I pulled out my bloody hand as I heard the other soldiers coming toward me. I could have been more tactical with my next approach, but I didn't have the time for that. I ran toward the soldiers. They were expecting it. They didn't expected me to run. My compound eyes kicked into gear and I saw the bullets coming from every corner, which allowed me to dodge them as I got to them. I threw an uppercut at the first soldier, flinging her 12 feet into the air. I rolled onto the ground as the other soldier attempted to shoot me. I grabbed her by the feet and used her like a golf club to sweep the third soldier off her feet. As both soldiers dropped to the ground, I sprung up into the air and landed on their heads, smashing them. The soldier I gave the uppercut to threw a knife at my back; I quickly turned, caught it and threw it back into the middle of her head, killing her instantly.

I walked out of the forest and met Soldier Red. She was standing in the driveway, her submachine gun placed at her feet.

"Are they all dead?" she asked. I nodded my head. "You are better than I thought. The general wanted all of us to come get you. I convinced him that 10 of us would get the job done, especially with me at the helm."

"Where is my father?"

"Don't misunderstand the gun on the ground. This is not me surrendering; it's me giving you the respect you deserve." She used her hand to gesture to me to approach and bounced on the ground like she was Mohammed Ali. I approached her; I wanted to end this charade. I threw the first punch and she dodged it, while throwing a punch at my face. The punch felt like a tap, but it was a valiant effort. She kept bouncing, proud of herself, as she thought her strategy was having an effect. I threw three punches at her and, each time, she dodged them with inhuman speed and returned punches hitting my face. I was getting irritated and she was getting pompous. I didn't have time for this, so I rushed at her. She leapt 10 feet in the air. I leapt up, caught her mid-air and bashed her face with my forehead, which ended her showboating. As we landed on the ground, I introduced her face to the four knuckles on my fist, which destabilized any hopes she had of walking away from me.

I stood over her. Her face bleeding and she was in pain, but she was not screaming, not even groaning although her physiognomy showed the pain. So, I stomped on her right knee, breaking it. Her eyes lit up with the expression of agonizing pain, but not a sound came from her lips.

"Where is my father?" I asked.

She took a phone from her pocket. Her hands were shaking, not out of fear, but from the damage I had done to her body. She pressed a speed dial number and handed me the phone. It was ringing and, then, someone picked up. "Eve," the woman said. "I am First Lieutenant Kwan. The omission of Captain Bubba's voice confirms that she is dead, dying or about to die. We are at a four mile attitude with your father flying to an undisclosed location. A mile away, there is a grey station wagon. Underneath the driver's seat is an iPad. The password is 7341. In the notes app is a note titled 'Origins,' which contains instructions as to what you are to do."

"I will make her talk," I said.

"Three things are certain. First, you will do what we ask you to do or your father will die. Second, Captain Bubba will die. And, finally, Captain Bubba will never talk." Then, she hung up.

I looked at the woman on the ground. She was trying to roll to her knees so that she could attempt to stand, but her left knee was unable to carry her body weight, so she fell back onto the ground. The regal soldier who had first engaged me into hand-to-hand combat was now reduced to a pathetic invalid. I knew she wouldn't talk, so I headed toward the car.

"Where are you going?" she asked. I looked back at her and didn't say a word. "Aren't you going to try and make me talk?" she asked as she continued to try to pull herself up with her arms. It was pointless giving her my time, so I kept walking down the driveway. "Kill me!" she ordered, but I kept on walking. "Please kill me!" I continued to ignore her and kept on walking.

I found the grey station wagon by the road leading to the house; I broke the windows and unlocked the car. I checked under the seat and found a brown manila envelope. In it was the iPad. I entered the password and checked the notes. Just then, I heard a single gunshot. Captain Bubba had crawled to her gun and shot herself.

Senator Dakota Knox

I drove 15 miles away from the closest town to a dingy bar in New Mexico. I walked in escorted by my four suited bodyguards. There was only one door in and one door out. I doubted whether the bungalow had ever past a health inspection. The place was made out of wood; the creaking sound could be heard throughout the place. It looked like a bar in a third world country, causing the electricity in the bar to seem out of place. I had on a dark grey pantsuit with flat heels. The bar was empty except for the non-English speaking bartender and Adam. There were wooden benches by wooden tables, the floor was dirty, the tables weren't clean and the ugly green wooden walls seemed to have blood stains on them. It was the perfect place to get lost. Adam sat with his head on the table, six bottles of empty Budweiser on the table in front of him. He had on cargo shorts and a worn-out grey shirt.

"I know for a fact that you are too young to drink," I said using my handkerchief to clean the bench before sitting opposite him.

He looked up at me and smiled, "In my defense, he didn't ask me for my ID."

"It's 10:30 in the morning. If he asked you for an ID in a place like this, I'd have been shocked."

He twirled an empty beer bottle, "I don't understand how anyone can become an alcohol addict; beer tastes like crap."

"You are young. When you get older, your sorrows will make it taste like honey," I said. Then, I put my hand over my nose, as a hobo walked into the bar. My security was quick to pay for his drink and kick him out of the room.

"You know how I found you?" I asked.

"The same way everyone else is tracking me via the chip by my heart."

"Everyone else?" I asked.

"Did you know about her?" he asked, looking me in the eyes.

"Who is her?" I asked, genuinely curious.

"Talk about leaving you in the dark," the teenager said, knowing from my reaction that I didn't know what he was talking about.

"I'm sure you will generously get me up to speed," I said.

"Why should I?"

"Because…" I leaned closer to him, "we both know Coriolanus. If you are not with him, you are against him."

"They arrested him."

I smirked, "Really, Adam? You and I know that man better than any one of those stupid lawmakers. Steel bars can't stop him from doing what he believes he has to do."

"Why are you bothered?"

"I drew first blood," I said.

His eyes brightened. "Do tell?" he said.

I looked at my security team and they immediately understood my meaning. They gently walked the bartender out of his bar. He gave slight protests, but some financial restitution helped with his change of heart.

When the room was empty, I spoke, "I architected the Jeremy Wong expose."

"And you are telling me this because…"

"Shouldn't your question be why I did it?"

"I have always been an egotistical cad."

I looked around the room, "Jeremy Wong was found hours ago, burnt to ashes. General Shockley has disappeared as well as every single member of the T-soldiers."

"Shockley was in on it?"

"Yes," I sighed at the thought of the information that he might have divulged if he was tortured. "You were in close proximity with the T-soldiers. Beyond Coriolanus, nobody knows as much of them as you. Is their loyalty to the American Flag or-"

"It's to Coriolanus," he cut me off. "Even worse is the Chameleon Project."

"What the hell is the Chameleon Project?" She sighed and quickly asked another question. "Should I be worried?"

"Yes, you should. If the T-soldiers are coming after you, you either have to kill them or they will kill you. They never retreat from a mission. You should know this."

"No, I don't. Congress cut funding for the project over 10 years ago. I wasn't aware they existed until Shockley revealed to me that Coriolanus had been funneling funds to take care of special projects all of these years. The fool thought he was embezzling and hoped to use that to blackmail him someday."

"What a pity. For the record, the only reason that you're alive is because they couldn't find you. Outside the building is a T-soldier who has been tailing me. I was wondering why and now I know why."

"Why?"

"They wanted me to lead them to you," I said as I stood and headed toward the door.

"I wouldn't go out there if I were you," he said nonchalantly, but I knew he was serious. "They don't miss."

I leaned against the wall and called out my security team, "Ryan! Tyrone! Eddie! Eddie! Ryan!"

"Stop screaming their names. They are already dead," he said as he looked at me, bored. I marched back to him, taking my phone from my breast pocket. "Who are you calling?" he asked.

"911."

"Okay," he said, getting up and heading toward the door.

"What are you doing?"

"I'm leaving," he said insouciantly.

"You are going to leave me here to die?"

"Where is Darshak?"

"I don't know. I thought he was dead."

"You see, you can't help me."

"Yes, I can," I said. "I can get you out into the open and let the world know what happened under this president's administration. I can let the world know the evil cruelty that this administration was involved in. You will be a celebrity. The world will love you. You will be on every news channel."

He pondered my words for a few seconds and then said, "A celebrity…one moment." Then, he ran out the door with inhuman speed and I realized in that moment that I was alone. I was about to dial 911 and then remembered that I was a senator. The press would have a field day with this. What was I doing in this dingy bar in New Mexico with maybe four or five dead bodies? I couldn't think of a credible excuse. Once this got out, I might as well kiss my presidential chances goodbye. This incident would have made Ted Kennedy's car accident look like a trivial story. At this moment, all I had to hope on was Adam. I could see the finish line; all I had to do was survive this moment. Everything was falling into place. The liberal wing of the Democratic Party had started going after the president, blaming him for escalating the torture system. The Republicans, true to form, had begun to attack the president because it was an excuse to go after him. James Luger was becoming a serious candidate from the Democratic Party and he was publicly flirting with the idea of challenging the president on the Democratic ticket. An anonymous $1 million donation from one of my subsidiaries helped anchor his decision to run. Winning the Republican nomination was almost certain. I had enough dirt on all the Republican candidates that my party would beg me to take the nomination.

Adam walked in with blood on his shirt. He sat back on the bench and didn't look at me, "So, you'll make a celebrity out of me?"

"Is it safe?" I asked.

"Yes, they are all dead. She killed all of your guards and I killed her," he replied, bored.

The boy referred to the death of humans as though he were killing weeds in a lawn. Getting my composure back I asked, "And the bartender?"

"She didn't kill him. He's still running for his life."

"Can you please go out there and kill him!?" I asked.

"Nah, I don't kill civilians."

I plodded to and fro, thinking of what my next move should be. I was scratching my head thinking of answers to obvious questions. Why was I here? Why had they wanted me dead? Who wanted me dead? I couldn't figure out how to explain it to the press. I needed to get away from here and disassociate myself from this mayhem. The only problem was the bartender. He could identify me, match me with my security detail. The bartender had to die. In that moment, I looked at Adam who still had a bored expression on his face and I smiled. Politics was a beautiful thing. Everything fell into place; the facts were clear. This was an assassination attempt by a female officer on a United States senator. I could see myself reading the eulogies of my security team members. I could see the justification for my presidency. It would be the perfect reason for why I decided to run for president. My stand against the president's oppressive democratic administration would be the motive for the attempt on my life and Adam would be the reason I was here, the one who saved me, the president's ugly secret and everything else that doesn't make sense in between. I was going to be president, I could taste it.

Oscar Perez

I love everything about my job. I am a 42–year-old Mexican-American, whose job, every day, is to make sure that nothing harmful gets past me to the most important man in the world: POTUS. The news said that some of my colleagues, fellow senior secret service agents, were killed in an assassination attempt on Senator Knox. She barely survived. Amongst them was Ryan Thomas. He and I were part of the secret service team assigned to protect the Iranian president 10 years ago; I was the senior agent on that detail. He was a professional, a father of two children like me; a good man. Like me, he loved what he did. Our wives did not fully understanding why anyone beyond our families should have the sacrifice of our lives before them. I had to keep telling my wife that it's a job and that's when things hit the fan. I told her that I wasn't going to take a bullet for anyone except her and the kids; it was a blatant lie and she knew it, but she appreciated the fact that I was telling it. My job was my life. I am a lean compact 5 foot 11 inches and am 190 pounds; a walking lethal weapon trained in eight forms of martial arts.

I was temporarily assigned to the president when he was a candidate for the presidency. We talked for barely a minute about the way I knotted my tie and, after that, he went out of his way to make my assignment to him permanent. He was my president and friend. I didn't expect it the other way around, but almost every day he asked about my wife and children by name; the gesture was so simple, but it meant the world to me. There is no better feeling than to know that the person you would take a bullet for is worth your life. I had protected a lot of disgusting human beings from foreign countries as well as domestic congressman and senators who preached one way in public and were engaged in despicable actions in private. It was a defined fact that the secret service never shared anything we saw, good or bad, a model that always brought us in contention with both the FBI and CIA.

There were 299 people on the president's detail. I and three other agents were with him in the Cadillac-badge limousine, otherwise known as The Beast. The president was sitting in the back, talking on the phone and reading papers. I and one of my colleagues sat opposite him, the other two were in front, one driving and the other in the passenger seat. Earlier in the day, after the president had been briefed on the assassination attempt on Senator Knox, the secret service tried to no avail to get the president to postpone his open speech to the students at the University of Southern California. He basically asked us if there was any verifiable threat of an assassination or wedding, which in plain English means a terrorist attack. When we said no, he adamantly maintained the appointment. We were all dressed for work in dark suits, light-blue shirts and red ties. I had a slight, artificial paunch around the middle, the result of my gun. The 10 freeway leading to the university was in a POTUS freeze for the president's motorcade. There were 20 cars in the two part motorcade and, we were in the secured package; two limousines heavily guarded by local law enforcement and the secret service. Hovering above us was the Marine One helicopter.

It seemed like a normal day and then I heard chatter from the radio transmitter about an unidentified object miles away on another freeway. Ten seconds later, I felt the weight of something hit the roof of the car. The driver quickly lost control of the wheel. I heard bullets firing as I dove on the president using my body to shield him from whatever was coming from the roof. As the car swerved, I felt the weight of whatever it was on the roof, punch through the roof of the car, causing the roof to dent and break the bulletproof glass on the sides. The other agent had pulled out his weapon and pointed it at the top of the car. That there was anything strong enough to dent The Beast shocked us all. The agent in the passenger's seat stuck his head out of the window to fire some shots, but, instead, I saw the hand of the creature, grab him by the arm and fling him out of the car. As the thing punched through the roof, the other agent in the backseat began firing at it, but it swatted away the bullets like they were flies. Then, it grabbed the agent and flung him out of the car. I didn't bother to look at the creature; I just grabbed the president, kicked the door open with both feet and jumped out of the car.

We landed hard on the freeway and rolled down the road. The car behind us in the motorcade had to swerve to avoid hitting us. The president's limousine swerved and bashed through the railings before crashing with the creature inside it. A throng of armed secret service agents and cops surrounded us as Marine One quickly landed beside the tight circle we made protecting the president. Just then, I saw it coming; it was a hairy beast. My fellow secret service agents quickly loaded the president into the helicopter and it flew off. Over 150 armed law officials began unleashing bullets at the creature as it moved at inhuman speeds toward us. The bullets seemed to bounce off it as it leapt over us unto a car, and jumped from car to car. Then, it leapt high into the air and caught the landing wheels of the Marine One. I ran, firing my weapon at the beast until I had to reload.

Then, I reloaded and kept firing, not caring that I was out of range. The helicopter kept going higher as three other helicopters followed it. When it was far away, I saw something drop out of it. I didn't know for certain what it was, I just knew that I had lost the president. I had failed in my duties. I had failed my country. I had failed my president.

General Coriolanus Cole

The secretary of defense was sweating profusely as he stood behind the steel cage separating him from me. In his present state of agitation, I realized that he was a much shorter man that I perceived. I had always known that he was 5 foot 6 inches tall, but he was always so composed and contained so much power that he seemed taller. Now, he seemed his normal height.

"How could you, Coriolanus?" he asked, his inner white shirt drenched in sweat.

I remained still, sitting on the bed. At the other end of the bed was a toilet and the sink was in between the two. "As you can see, Secretary O'Neill, I have been in here the entire time."

"That's my point! You're in here without any TV or Internet access, yet you seem to know everything that's going on!"

"Isn't it pathetic how quickly the stock markets can crash with the slightest news?" I asked, rubbing my stubby chin. I needed a shave.

"No one who loves their country would ever do this! No one!"

"Stop screaming, Secretary O'Neill. You're deafening me," I said, rubbing my ears.

"This is the stupidest thing anyone, especially you, could have pulled. You would have gotten a slap on the wrist and a dishonorable discharge, now you'll get the chair."

"Dishonorably discharged," I said and stood up, closing the distance between us. "The army is my life. If you think that I care about death, then you are bigger fool than all of them combined. I gave my blood, my youth, my life for the army, for this country and what did they do? Those parasites who sucked on the protection that I provided dared to call me a traitor."

"It was a few people with that notion."

"I saw the polls!" I yelled as I banged on the steel bars. "Seventy-five percent of Americans thought I should be locked up for catching and beating information out of a terrorist, a terrorist whose sole purpose was to kill Americans."

"And the other 25%? They don't count?"

I smirked, "I was the butt of all the jokes on late night TV. Are they still laughing now? Now that the world has seen America's weakness?"

"Is this what you wanted? To verify yourself as a traitor. Is this what you want?!"

"No..." I dragged out the word, maintaining eye contact. "I want more."

"You are insane," Secretary O'Neill said as he stepped back.

"No, Mr. Secretary, I am in control," I said as I turned my back to him and walked back to my bed. "Right about now, they are considering swearing in the Vice President. Please make sure that you tell him that if he accepts the nomination that we will go into the White House and pick him out like a leach." I lay down on the bed. "You have until 9 AM Eastern Standard Time to get me out of here and lodge me in the Hotel Barceló Marina Palace in Varadero, Cuba. The room I will be staying in has already been arranged with everything I need to address the nation live in time for the morning news. You better make sure that I and my brothers-in-arms are able to view the broadcast live on NBC, ABC, CBS and Fox."

"And if we don't do what you ask?"

"Really, Mr. Secretary," I said, looking at him as I lay on the bed. "We are only good at protecting ourselves from what we understand and, in this case, you have no idea what you are dealing with."

He took a deep breath and said, "You might need to give me more time."

"The live broadcast is the only way that I can prevent the death of the president. Also, one more thing, General Lance Shockley's body is buried by your dog's kernel." He stared at me, confused. "Now, now, move on. You have a lot of work to do." Then, I closed my eyes, enjoying every moment of my revenge.

"This is an unprecedented event. We can beat the information out of you," he said. I could feel his eyes on me.

"There were over a thousand probabilities of things that will or could happen. Did you not think I factored that into my train of thought? Like, for instance," I sat up and looked at him, "how did I know that you would know it was me?"

"I didn't. I just conned you into confessing."

"You didn't. When you walked in here, you knew the man I was would never carry out such a titanic expedition and hide behind lies. The only mistake you made was that you didn't use the same thought process when you let them put me in handcuffs," I said as I lay back down and closed my eyes. "What time is it?"

He remained taciturn for a while and I knew he was deliberating whether the information could be used to my advantage. Then, he said, "10:43."

"You poor soul, you've been up all night. Cuba is over 11 hundred miles away. If I were you, I would run along. Time is wasting and you have less than 10 hours to prepare the nation for me."

EVE

2:10 AM

I was in an abandoned hovel in the Sonoran Desert of Arizona. The wood was discolored and the place was dusty, empty and abandoned. I doubted if anyone had been there in the last decade. We were completely surrounded by desert sands and cactus plants. The instructions I was given had directed me to take the president to a bunker in the Sonoran Desert, 59 miles away from the nearest town. On my way there, I saw this cabin and diverted the land rover I was driving. I hoped and prayed that I hadn't killed anyone when I got the president. When the helicopter was in the air, I jumped and climbed in. I knocked out the president, grabbed him, deflecting the bullets the secret service agents were firing at me and jumped off the helicopter in midair with him. As I landed, I began digging a tunnel downwards, while dragging the unconscious president. When I dug out, I went to the land rover they had waiting for me close to the train tracks. In it was a change of clothing for the president. I had to undress the man completely, throw his clothes at the incoming train and dress him in a track suit. The track suit had a scrambler in it to prevent any tracker they had inserted into his body, from working. Driving to the desert was a breeze. Nobody stopped us. When I got to the hovel, I could have kept going, but I chose to stop. I knew once they had the president, there would be no incentive for them to give my father back.

The president lay asleep opposite me. The flooring in the hovel was dilapidated and it was a miracle that it was still standing. It was 15 feet long, 15 feet wide and 18 feet tall. The best part was the roofing, which seemed solid compared to the rest of the structure. The president and I were both dressed in matching track suits with Jordan sneakers.

There were bullets in me; I noticed them every time I tightened my muscles, I was able to push the bullets out, but it was an excruciating painful process and I didn't want to wake the man. It was bad enough that, in one moment, I helped him create history by being the first America president to be kidnapped.

Something in my skin kept bubbling. I felt my pores opening and closing and each time the pores got bigger. My body was trying to start creating a cocoon, but I couldn't let it. I needed to be awake and aware of everything until I found my father. It was more painful fighting my body from entering the cocoon state than it was pushing out the bullets. My writhing woke him and he looked at me, not with fear, but with some kind of pity.

"Are you okay?" he asked me.

The question broke my heart. I had just kidnapped him and here he was asking me if I was okay. "Yes," I answered, hoping that he was mentally screwing with my head.

He sat up, rubbing his neck and jaw, "Where are we?"

"Arizona."

"So much for the Arizonan border control," he said. I couldn't help, but laugh, he was funny. "So, it would be smart if we got out of here before that creature comes back?"

At that point, I realized what he was doing. He was trying to get me comfortable, so that he could help rescue me from the creature that kidnapped him. "I am the creature," I replied.

He looked at me confused, pondering what to say. "Has anyone told you that you look like my daughter, just a little shorter?"

Now, I was confused, but I answered the question anyway. "I get it all the time," I responded, "but thank goodness for the accent. It helps to geographically distinguish us."

"I know the accent. Don't tell me... it's West African."

"Yes, Nigerian."

"Whatever you tell me, don't tell me it was a Nigerian invasion," he said. It was a serious statement, but, the way he said it, it came out funny and I started laughing.

"No, sir," I replied. He looked around the place and then at his tracksuit. "Sorry, I had to change you."

"Not a problem," he said and then stood up. Then, he remembered he wasn't the president, but was a hostage. He looked at me, "Do you mind?"

"Sure, you can stand, walk around, even run away. We are completely surrounded by the desert," I said, trying to sound funny, but it came out more intense than I wanted.

He said nothing, just looked around the place at the wide gaps between the wooden walls. He rested his hands on the frame and sighed.

"Is something wrong?"

"It's just so peaceful here," he said as he walked out the door.

I remained in the hovel for a little bit. I felt weak and I tried to maintain my composure as I fought with my body. Eventually, I walked out and found the president sitting on the sand behind the car, looking into the quiet sky. It was 38 degrees at night, much cooler than it was when I arrived.

"Can I join you?"

He looked up at me and said, "As long as you're not a member of congress."

"No, I'm not," I said with a smile. We sat together on the sand for close to five minutes not saying a word, just looking into the sky. Finally, I said, "I will not let them hurt you."

He looked at me and smiled. Then, he turned and looked back up into the sky.

The silence was comforting, but my guilt couldn't let me remain quiet. "I thought you'd try to break into the car, hotwire it and attempt to escape."

"The key word young lady is attempt," he said. Then, he turned to me, "I saw you as a hairy monster breaking into a bulletproof limousine. You ran faster than the cars coming toward me. You leapt over cars like the incredible hulk and then you flew into the air and caught a helicopter. Now, here you are, undetectable with the might of the entire United States searching for you. After experiencing all of that, I do not think it logical to attempt to escape."

"Are you afraid?"

"Of you?" he asked, arching his eyebrows.

"Yes," I said, feeling ashamed.

"No. Have you heard of the Cartesian split?"

"Yes, it's the moment when rational, scientific knowledge is separated from feelings or intuitive knowledge."

"Exactly," he said as he placed his hand on my shoulder. "When you meet as many people as I have and shaken as many hands as I have, you learn a lot from the vibes people give."

"I have excellent vibes."

"Now, now, now, don't get ahead of yourself," he said. We both laughed. "I do get afraid; that's why I pray a lot. I pray my daughters don't face the same kind of prejudice I have been exposed to. I pray that they don't end up with spouses who make them unhappy. I pray that I leave the country better than I found it. I pray that more Americans don't die senseless deaths."

"Are you saying all of this to get me to let you go?" I asked with a mocking expression.

He smiled warmly, "I know you want to, but you can't and I understand."

"They have my father."

He gently tapped my back. "Everything will be alright." Then, he walked back toward the hovel.

"Thank you," I said.

"For what? Using a line that I use on all of my constituents facing hard times."

"For not asking me what I am... and talking to me the same way you would talk to any other... human being."

He said nothing and just smiled and entered the hovel.

My cell phone rang. I knew it was them. I had ignored their calls for the last three hours. Now, I knew it was time to face the tiger. I picked it up and didn't say anything.

"You were supposed to bring mama home," the voice I recognized as Lieutenant Kwan said. The president was mama.

"I want to see my teacher first," I said. They had given me a list of codenames in the envelope. My father was the teacher and the bunker was home.

"Your teacher is home. Come with mama and we can have an exchange of toys," she said.

"No," I replied.

"We know where you are," Lieutenant Kwan said.

"I know. So, bring the teacher here to me and you can take mama."

"We can't just come around. Too many eyes are out there looking for mama. We will attract the hyenas," she said.

"That's the point. Under present circumstances, you'll come light to the party."

"Due to the present circumstances, we can only take baby steps to you. We will be there at 8. Leave the line open; I will call back," she said, hanging up the phone.

I looked back at the car. I knew there was a tracker in it, but I didn't care. From my present location, I could see for miles around. The only thing I was worried about was myself. I was getting weak. I needed to sleep, but I couldn't sleep. If I closed my

eyes, I knew I would fall into a cocoon state and father's life would be in their hands. I needed to stay awake. I was the only reason father was still alive. My skin was beginning to swell from absorbing water moisture in the air. I was weak, but I was going to stay awake. I had to stay awake.

Adam

3:45 AM

I had spent the night at Senator Knox's home. The room I was sleeping in was depressingly pink and full of knick-knacks in vieux saxe. It was the kind of room that a stupid teenage girl who thinks love will make everything perfect would decorate. The sheets, drapes and rug were all white. I hated the room, but the bed was extremely comfortable. I wasn't aware when I had dozed off before the senator came in screaming.

"Four hours!" Knox screamed, waking me up as she tore open the blinds, looking into the dark morning. "Four hours is all I had before that bastard had to let himself get kidnapped and steal the spotlight." Something was wrong. Normally my snakelike infra-red sensors detected people a mile away, but I didn't even notice her come in. This had happened the last time I saw her in New Mexico as well.

I sat up confused as to why I didn't sense her. "Sorry, Dakota."

"Dakota," she said the word in disgust. Then, she marched toward me. "You will refer to me as Senator Dakota Knox, Senator Knox or mother if that will make you feel better." I looked at her as though she was insane. "You need to tell me about this girl."

"Why would I call you mother?" I asked, fascinated.

"Oh, that," she said flippantly. "We were monitoring Darshak's experiment and we knew his artificial egg process wasn't going to work, especially after Kozlov confirmed it, so, when he wasn't aware, I got another doctor on the staff to switch the eggs with mine. We need to find the president before anyone else."

I looked at her with my mouth open; I wasn't sure if she was crazy or trying to manipulate me. "Are you joking?"

"No, I am not. There is no way we can beat a kidnapped president. It will be a landslide if I go against him, and if I have to wait after his second term, that's another six years. Six years is a lifetime. We have only one choice left, we-"

"We!?" I jumped in front of her. My head was over her head. The webbed wing from my elbow to my waist had torn open my t-shirt. The quills didn't shoot out, but I was angry. I noticed that my feet weren't touching the ground as I floated above her.

She looked deep into my angry red eyes without a trace of fear and said, "Yes, we, mother and son."

I could have killed her. I should have killed her. "You're lying," I said.

"Believe what you want to believe," she said as she walked to the window. "Tell me about this girl. Are you and her similar in every way?"

I didn't know how she was doing it, but I was quickly trapped by the maternal field a mother has over her children. "Yes," I replied.

"The president is isolated, probably with this girl or the T-soldiers. We will need to find him and kill him before anyone else gets him."

"We...as in me," I responded.

"All of these years, who do you think has been on Coriolanus to let you roam the planet doing what you want to do? As soon as the T-soldiers didn't want to kill each other, he wanted you eliminated. I fought to keep you alive, then and now. Even Darshak is alive because I knew you needed him alive. Why do you think DC never knew about you? Not even the president knew about you because I was the wing that shielded you from the vultures that would have devoured you. All these things I did for you. I didn't ask for a thank you. Now, for the first time in your existence, I am personally asking for a favor… from a mother to her son."

I didn't believe the words I was hearing from a woman I had known all my life as a ruthless boss; suddenly she was talking to me as my mother. She could have been lying, but I knew she wasn't.

"If I kill him, that would make me a terrorist," I said, awed by the words coming out of my mouth.

"That's a harsh word to use."

"A terrorist is a person who uses terrorism in the pursuit of political aims," I retorted as I sat back on the bed.

She sighed and sat next to me. "You don't have to do it. It just feels good to be able to call you son. You will never know how good it makes me feel." She kissed my forehead and then got up and headed for the door. "Go back to bed. I need to introduce you to my husband during breakfast. We should just tell him that I gave you up for adoption and you found me."

She was manipulating me. I knew it, but I was already caught in her web, "If I want to do this and I am not saying I will do it."

"Sure, you won't," she replied matter-of-factly.

"How would we know where he is?" I asked.

"The T-soldiers, like you, have a tracker in them. Only Coriolanus and Darshak have access to this information."

"You found Darshak."

"Yes, we did," she said. Then, she looked puzzled. "Who hides out in Vegas?"

"Darshak," I said smiling to myself.

"He's in a hotel a few miles away. You want me to bring him here?"

"Nah," I said. It was odd. I'd always wanted him safe, but I never really liked being around him. The general was right; I saw him like a pet, someone I owned. "Did he tell you where they are?"

"Even better, he gave us the tracker."

I brooded over my next words. "If you are telling me the truth, which I don't believe, then you are not my mother. You are just an egg donor. Do you understand that?"

"No, I don't understand that. You were born of my egg. You are my son. My DNA lives in you. If you don't want to get involved in my situation, that's acceptable, but facts are facts. You are mine and I will never stop knowing of you as my son."

"Where was this maternal commitment all of those years I spent alone growing up?"

"I was always with you. I never let you out of my sight."

I began clapping my hands and talking sarcastically. "Isn't it the mother of the year? The mother who puts a tracker in my heart."

"A mother has to watch her young."

"A mother who never hesitated to let the army throw me into Iran, North Korea, Somalia, Russia and over 300 missions that put my life on the line."

She smirked and said, "That's what you live for. If I came between you and your adrenaline kick, then I would have been your greatest enemy." She sighed, "Why do you think you got more attached to Coriolanus than you were to Darshak? I know you because my blood flows in your veins." She abruptly straightened up, as though an emperor had walked into the room. "Wash up and come down. We have a lot to discuss." She walked out the room and it hit me, she knew me, more than I knew myself.

Secretary O'Neill

4:13 AM

I was against water boarding and all forms of torture; POTUS was even more adamant against it, but extraordinary circumstances give birth to extreme solutions. I stood behind the two way mirror, watching Coriolanus who had his hands tied behind his back. His legs were tied to the bottom of the chair and he only wore his underwear. He was bleeding from several wounds on his body, but his face hadn't been touched. There was a big bucket of water in the room and other object. The two colossal men inflicting the pain on him were named Eric and Ryan. They were both tall, had hard faces and with veins that lined their hard muscles. Eric was black and Ryan was white.

Eric squatted down next to Coriolanus, who was trying to breath. "Tell us where the president is and I promise you it will be over."

Coriolanus' head had fallen down. He was too weak after the down pour of blows to keep it up. He said, in almost a whisper, "I am General Coriolanus Cole-" Before he could finish his statement, Eric landed blows on his ribs.

He writhed in pain as Eric stood over him, "Will you talk now?"

Coriolanus replied, "Time is running out."

Ryan grabbed him by the back of his neck, his massive hands converging around his neck. He dragged both him and the chair to the bucket; his head faced the ground as his knees scraped the floor. Ryan dunked Coriolanus's head into the bucket. Coriolanus wiggled in the chair as he drowned. Ryan held him there for 15 seconds and then pulled him out.

As soon as Coriolanus got out of the water, he coughed water from his nose and mouth and gasped for air.

"Where is the president?!" Ryan screamed at him, with his face right in front of his, holding the back of his neck, with only two legs of the chair resting on the floor.

Coriolanus gasped for more air and then looked at Ryan and smiled. This gesture vexed him and Ryan vehemently dumped him back into the bucket.

I wasn't aware that Eric had left the room and joined me. "It's been over four hours; he is not going to talk."

"Everyone cracks," I said.

"He isn't everyone," Eric said. "He is General Coriolanus Cole."

I couldn't believe this was happening, "20 more minutes and then try electrocution."

"And if he still doesn't talk?"

I sighed, "Clean him up and get him ready for TV." I walked to the door and then stopped, "And remember, don't touch his face. We wouldn't want to give the wrong impression."

Lieutenant Kwan

7:54 AM

Before I joined the army what bothered me most was that people automatically thought I was South Korean because of my name. When I did correct them about my Chinese ancestry, I was automatically labeled as a spy in their heads. It sucked so bad that I joined the army just to prove a point to them. I excelled as a soldier; it was where I was supposed to be. When General Coriolanus Cole recruited me to be a second-tier volunteer for the Restart Program, I felt insulted that I wasn't chosen with the first selections until he explained to me that the first two volunteers were the scapegoats to check to see if the program worked. If it did, and it did, I was to head the second batch. The experiment succeeded and the first two soldiers experimented on became super soldiers, which inevitably pushed all second-tier volunteers; ranks below the first two T-soldiers. When they finally got around to the second-tier volunteers, there was too much jealousy amongst us. We practically hated each other, but our loyalty to the army never wavered. With time, our hatred grew, but, when we started changing, it suddenly dissipated. During the change, my chest began to protrude out breasts; the hair on my body, except my hair on my head, fell out;

my phallus began to shrink; and the meatus opened wide enough to become a vagina. The metamorphosis took four months, four painful months, but, after that, I understood completely what I was to do with my life and that was to give my undivided loyalty to my commanding officer.

The orders were simple, if General Coriolanus Cole was arrested, we were to kill everyone who knew any specific details about the Restart programs except Doctor Lin. Then, we were to kidnap Professor Kozlov and hand him over to Doctor Lin. We were to get the girl to kidnap the president for her father and then get the president and hold him until the general gave us a signal on live TV to either kill him or let him go. Everything was going according to plan, with the exception of the few comrades we lost on the way. As much as we told ourselves that we were doing this because the general was our direct commanding officer, it was more. We watched him on TV sacrifice his career and freedom for one of us, and I and every T-soldier knew that the man was worthy of our deaths.

Our three hummers were parked around the hovel in the middle of the desert. I got out of the car with Professor Kozlov; the man was treated like an egg because we knew that Eve wasn't someone we wanted to test, unless we had to. We were eight in total, including the professor who stood around the house.

Two soldiers were in the back and five us stood with the professor in front of the entrance. We stood in front of the land rover and waited. We knew she was in there and she knew we were outside. We were closer than 50 meters, enough distance to make sure our submachine guns didn't miss their targets when shot. I could have called out her name, but there was a certain tension in the air. It was 85 degrees; the Arizona heat had started causing us to sweat. She wasn't coming out; the other soldiers looked at me, waiting for a signal as to whether we should go in or wait outside. I just stood with my eyes on the hovel. There were sand dunes, saguaro cacti and creosote bushes all over the desert. Even with the heat, it was windy, causing the sand to be picked up and tossed around, creating a minor sand storm. A bighorn sheep stood a distance away, watching us, as though expecting a show. Tactically forcing our way into the hovel was not a good idea. The girl had killed the best of us and, until we got the order from the general, the president was to remain alive. I wanted to call out her name, but there something that didn't feel right about it, especially as we had her father. So, we just waited patiently for her to make the first move.

EVE

My conscience was screaming louder than I could bear to hear. I knew this was wrong. I felt it in every cell of my body. Using the life of my father as excuse for handing over another human to be slaughtered didn't feel right, but, then again, they wouldn't kill him, they needed him alive.

The president stood in front of me and said, "Your friends are here."

"They are not my friends."

"We shouldn't keep them waiting," he said in hurry to get out of the hovel.

"They are early, so they can wait," I said pacing angrily. "Am I doing the right thing?" I asked, pleading with him to ease my conscious.

"You are doing what you have to do for the one you love. You own no part of the blame," he said, putting his hand on my shoulder. It felt like a warm blanket in the cold.

Tears sipped down my face as I said, "I am so sorry."

"It's going to be alright," he said, consoling me, as though I was the one who had been captured. He wiped the tears from my eyes and said, "Take it from me, the only serving presidents that Americans really love are dead presidents."

"They won't kill you," I quickly replied.

"You're right. They need me alive. I was just being comical," he said.

I sighed. I was in a lot of pain; my body was so weak. I needed sleep. My body needed to heal, but I couldn't let them see my weakness. I put my hand to my waist and looked at the president. He gave me a nod of approval and we both walked out the hovel to meet the soldiers.

Lieutenant Kwan

8:03 AM

Eve walked out with the president, thanks to the privilege of battle; I could spot a wounded adversary, even if the adversary was a giant. She was weak, her steps were heavy; this person was either an imposter or a much weaker person than the one who killed Captain Bubba and the other T-soldiers. She was black and skinny with curly afro hair. She was young, very young. I expected a veteran and not a teenager. What confused me was the president; he seemed very comfortable with the situation. It was almost as if he planned the whole thing himself. This was a once in a lifetime chance. If there was any hope of killing something like Eve, it was now, when she was broken.

"Eve," I said acknowledging her.

"Lieutenant Kwan," she replied in kind.

"You took your time coming out," I said sarcastically.

"You were early," she replied with a straight face.

"Mr. President," I said with a respectful nod.

He looked back at me and said, "Lieutenant."

"Are you okay, dad?" Eve asked the professor.

"I'm fine," Professor Kozlov responded, standing between me and another soldier.

The two soldiers at the back of the house were laying flat on the ground, pointing their Cheytac .408 sniper rifles at Eve.

"I see we have ourselves a Mexican standoff," Eve said.

I looked around at the five soldiers by me. They had their guns on their shoulders, pointing them at the sky, "Why would you say that?"

"To get the president, I didn't have 10 or 20 bullets shot at me, I had hundreds. Six pierced me and I am still alive." Her focus was just on me, "The question is whether the two snipers behind me think that their bullets will reach me before I punch through their spines." The president quickly looked back and noticed the two snipers behind them, trying to blend in with the dirt.

I grinned, "The difference between us and the secret service is that we never miss."

"That depends on what you are shooting at," Eve said as she maintained eye contact with me. It seemed as though she wanted a confrontation. "Captain Bubba

and your other soldiers would have strongly disagreed, if they were still alive."

"The infra-red thing?" I asked, referring to her snakelike sensors that detected my soldiers without looking back.

"Yes," she answered.

I signaled the two soldiers and they walked from the back of the hovel to the front and stood behind me. "So, let's do this."

"One thing, you need to promise that you are not going to hurt him," Eve said. The question baffled me, but it seemed to be more of a surprise to her father.

My initial response was to tell her that her condition wasn't part of the deal, but I was dealing with a more superior individual, so respect was due. "We just want to use him to get what we want."

She remained taciturn, standing by the president 100 feet away from us. She was thinking and that wasn't good. She wasn't as weak as I thought. I wasn't sure what to do; if I gave the signal to attack, there was a high probability that we might all die, which wasn't an issue for me, but the mission was the priority. I had to be patient; she was a teenage girl looking for a way to vent.

She began kicking her sneakers into the Earth. I let her venting take its course as we waited for 60 seconds in wordless silence. Then, she said, "How are we going to do this?"

"The president walks to us as your father walks to you."

She continued tapping her shoes into the sand.

"Well?" I asked.

"I'm thinking," she replied, not looking at me, just standing with her hands behind her back, biting her lips and looking into the sky.

All of the soldiers looked at me, waiting for my order. This wasn't a youthful tantrum; it was a strategy. She was calling us out. She wanted us to make the first move. I was a woman who had never experienced being a teenage girl, so I couldn't understand what she was thinking. However, the best strategy I had now was not to do what she wanted us to do. So, we all stood under the burning Arizona morning sun waiting for her to make her move.

General Coriolanus Cole

8:03 AM

In my opinion, it was downright shameful how easy it was to get into Cuba. It, frankly, was harder to get into Canada from the United States and the Canadians are our allies. I was lodged in the suite ordered by my soldiers. The room had a live feed into a website that all the news channels had been informed would air my broadcast. The balcony of my room, which gave an excellent view of the ocean, was separated from the bedroom by a sliding glass door. The drapes were cream colored, along with the bed sheets on the king-sized bed. I was in the topmost room of the hotel. A sliver of the morning light shined upon me as I sat alone in the room, dressed in my full army attire, waiting to address the nation. The Cuban government wasn't aware of my intentions, but the CIA was. They had practically booked every vacant room in the hotel. My room was booked for a week prior to my arrival by my soldiers and the 'do not disturb' sign hung on the door handle during that time, ensuring that house cleaning didn't come in the room.

I checked my watch for the time and looked at the closed laptop I was going to use to transmit my speech. I touched my cufflinks, getting bored. I had to wait for another 45 minutes before I could get ready. I tried standing up, but the pain from the beatings I received earlier wouldn't let me. It was hell getting dressed as my ribs were broken and my legs fractured. However, I had enough strength to do what I had to do. It was a shame how the country I loved and I had to go our separate ways, but, the truth is raw, the ones you love deserve to be punished when they spit on your love. I put on the TV and the news showed that the world was going crazy about the president being kidnapped. Every channel in the world was talking about it. The country was going ballistic. The stock market was falling by the minute and everyone was taking their money from the banks in droves. The nature of the kidnap scared the world more than they could fathom. People were already buying bulk loads of food, preparing for Armageddon.

I heard a gentle knock on the door. The CIA knew better than to knock on the door because I was in Cuba and they couldn't easily get their hands on me. Also, with a kidnapped president, all rules had gone out the door. In the paranoid state of the White House, they would gladly bomb Cuba just to save face. I lumbered heavily on the parquet to the door, using the chair as support as I rolled it to the door. I looked through the keyhole and saw the most beautifully dressed soldiers waiting outside my door. I had to take a deep breath to gain my strength to face them.

I opened the door to meet them. Their uniforms were well–pressed and their shoes polished well enough to show my reflection. They were the same height as me. The older of the two men was in the marines and the younger was in the air force. They both chose not to join the army because they didn't want any preferential treatment because of their father. Their names were Kyle and Eli. Most people thought they were twins because they looked so much alike, except for their scars and the 10 pounds extra that Eli weighed. It was hard for any stranger to tell them apart.

"Father," Kyle said, standing outside the door.

"Kyle," I said with a warm smile. He attempted to smile back, but was unable to. "Eli."

Eli's response was sharp, "Is it true?"

"Come inside," I said beckoning them in. Kyle walked in, but Eli remained outside the door.

"Did you kidnap the president?" he asked from out the doorway.

"Remember who you are talking to," I said as I threw a warning gaze at him.

"That's the point, father. Who am I talking to? The man who raised me to live and die for my country

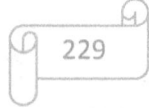

or the traitor who architected the kidnapping of the president?" Eli asked.

"Are you done?" I asked him.

"No, I am not."

"That's a pity," I said and I shut the door in his face. Kyle remained standing, looking at me, as tears streamed down his face. He didn't say anything and wasn't even aware that he was crying. This gesture hurt me deeper than the beating I had received earlier. I couldn't look at his eyes anymore, they had shame in them. I limped to my bed and sat down.

He followed me and sat by me. "Are you okay?" he asked.

"Yes," I touched my ribs and winced. "I fell down the stairs." He smiled and I knew that he understood.

"Guantanamo Bay?" he asked.

"D.C."

"Wow, you must have gotten everyone ballistics."

I sighed and then said, "Son-"

He put his hands on my lips and pointed at his chest. He was letting me know that he was wearing a wire. The beauty was that this son of mine, whose

father had betrayed the country he loved, was still going out of his way to protect his father. The gesture was too much to bear and I broke down crying. He didn't attempt to stop me; he just let me cry it all out.

"I am selfish," I said wiping off the tears. "I wanted every America punished for its shameful neglect of the people who protect her, who die for her, who bleed for her." I got up and walked to the sliding glass doors that lead to the balcony. "How is your mother?"

"She is not well. She is now the scorn of the same society that adored her," Kyle said.

"And this is because I didn't give up Soldier Red?" I laughed to myself. "How would they treat her if they knew I was behind the present calamity?"

"They might lynch her, me and Eli."

"I don't expect you to understand what I am doing, but I need you to never forget that there wasn't a day of my life that went by that I didn't think of you, your brother and your mother."

"I know," he replied.

I turned to him, "Why don't you scream at me!? Shout at me!? Why don't you call me a traitor like your brother?"

"Because…"

"Because of what!?" I screamed.

"You are my father."

He broke me.

"…And you are my son," I sighed. "Get me the phone by the desk drawer."

He got the phone by the drawer as I sat back on the bed. I dialed a number. The phone rang once and the person on the other end of the line quickly picked it up.

"Yes," Secretary O'Neill said.

"What's the deal?" I asked.

"You never come back to the United States," O'Neill said.

"And?" I asked.

"No one will ever know you were involved with the kidnapping, so your family wouldn't have to undergo any prosecutions…" O'Neill dragged out the word, his way of letting me know that they were listening in on me.

"And?" I asked.

There was a long pause and then he said, "$1 million."

"I was going for the full exoneration of Soldier Red, but I could do with a little extra change to buy myself a place. However, I have one more condition."

"Name it."

"The people who are holding the president. I want them all alive. You can hurt them, but I want them alive and exonerated when you get POTUS."

"You know how this works. We need a scapegoat; someone has to take the fall, especially with your name white-lined from the kidnapping."

"That's easy, put it on Shockley."

I could hear him whisper to others; he was probably in the war room with the president's cabinet. "You realize that if POTUS dies, then there is no deal," he said.

"I do, so you need to hurry up and get me the deal in writing."

He paused again and then said, "I have to take the offer to the vice president and cabinet."

"Listen to me. I need the deal in writing and you need to give it to me quickly. The president's life is in your hands," I said and then hung up.

"Will they make it on time?" Kyle asked, anxious.

I looked up at him and smiled, "Are you hungry?"

"No," he answered.

"Aren't you going to call your people to tell them the status of things?" Kyle asked.

I looked at him and then around the room, "After I get a copy of the contract, signed by the vice president and secretary of state."

Kyle looked at me weirdly as I talked to the room and then asked, "Are you talking to me?"

"No, son, I am talking to the room."

"Are you being sarcastic?"

"No, I'm being literal. The room is bugged." There was a knock at the door, "Please help me with the door."

Kyle walked to the door and opened it for a CIA agent wearing a Hawaii shirt and cargo pants. He walked straight to the bed, opened a briefcase containing a million dollars and three pages of stapled documents.

Kyle looked at me, amazed. "You just talked to them less than five minutes ago."

"Son," I said pulling out my pen and reading the contracts as I talked, "the document was already prepared before you got here. They knew what I wanted and they added the $1 million because they are marked bills. They can use it to trace me if I disappear."

"But he said he had to talk to the cabinet," Kyle asked, still confused.

"He was with the cabinet when he called," I said. Then, I stopped and looked at the agent, "The contract says nothing about my men not getting killed during the rescue."

"The fax was on its way. It will be here any second," he said. Just then another agent opened the door and entered, not bothering to check to see if the door was locked. He handed him the document, which he handed to me.

I read through the papers, signed them and gave them their copy. Then, I said, "Bunker 18950 in the

Sonoran Desert." As soon as I told them the information, the second agent ran out of the door.

I picked up my phone and made a call, while the agent started looking around my room. Lieutenant Kwan answered the phone and I said, "Let mama fly. There is going to be a party."

Then, the agent took the phone from me and said in a commanding tone, "No calls." He hung up the phone. His hands brushed by his gun holster tucked underneath his shirt. Eleven other CIA agents walked into the room, liked they owned it and me.

"I thought they made a deal?" Kyle asked, bewildered.

"The president isn't secured yet," the agent said, who was now, evidently, disgusted by my existence.

"Can I use the bathroom?" I asked like a child in kindergarten.

He looked to make sure that the money was still on the bed and then he walked ahead of me to the bathroom. I stood behind him with a bored expression on my face. The bathroom contained a shower with a floral shower curtain and walls plastered with porcelain tiles. The sink was juxtaposed to the toilet and the floor was tiled in marble. The agent walked out of the bathroom.

"So, is that a yes?" I asked.

He didn't say a word; he just used his fingers to give me permission to use the bathroom. As I walked pass Kyle, I touched his face. At that point, I didn't believe that there was a man who loved his son more than I did. I walked into the bathroom and closed the door behind me.

Lieutenant Kwan

8:19 AM

We had waited for over 15 minutes. The sun was getting hotter and Eve was still playing with her thoughts and digging her heels into the ground. I initially thought this was strategy and then I thought that she was just being a teenager. Then, I thought it was her wrestling with her conscience, but, now, I had no idea why this child was wasting my time. I couldn't take this anymore. My soldiers remained calm, focused and professional, waiting for any order I dished out. The president looked straight ahead through her awkwardness. Her father was the only one who seemed to appreciate what I was going through with her tardiness in decision-making. Professor Kozlov was sweating profusely, scared out of his mind, but his lips were sealed.

It was pointless. I couldn't wait any longer; I had to give the order. Just then, my phone rang and all eyes were on me. I looked around awkwardly, "Sorry, I have to get this."

I picked up the phone and, on the other end, was General Coriolanus Cole. He said, "Let mama fly. There is going to be a party."

That was the first command; we were to let the President go. Before he could give the other three commands, the line got cut off. A long shot desire was to kill her and get hair and blood samples. Eve was weak or she was pretending to be weak. If she was weak, there was a 50-50 chance that we could kill her or she could kill all of us. We had watched the tapes, the secret service and cops had loaded bullets in her, yet, here, she was, standing as though she was coming back from an eight hour desk job. The whole weakness thing must be a trick to get us to attempt to draw first blood, so she could take advantage of the situation. She was the same as that beast, Adam, who savored killing us because we were better targets than ordinary soldiers. I longed for the day when I killed that monster myself. I wasn't afraid; I was just logical. Phase 2 of the General's plan was more important than this phase and he needed at least 10 of us to survive. The only thing holding us back from bloodshed was her father. Once we gave the man over to her, we were all going to die, unless she really gave a damn about the president. I had to give the order and I had to give it now.

Eve

I literally fell asleep with my eyes open, standing next to the president. My body wasn't waiting for my brain anymore; it was taking matters into its own hands, so to speak. I didn't know what happened or where I was until I heard a phone ring and my brain jutted me back into control. Everyone seemed so tense. In the distance, I could hear a helicopter coming, someone must have found us, the question was who. Lieutenant Kwan didn't talk; she just listened to the person on the phone and then put it back into her pocket. I tried to put on a straight face. I wondered how long I had been out. I was hoping that it had only been a few seconds. I wasn't sure how to continue the conversation.

"Eve," Lieutenant Kwan said. "Let's make a deal. You get to keep your father and the president if you give us samples of your hair and blood."

"No!" The president spoke out loud, not in his usual composed manner. Father looked at him with disdain. He didn't appreciate someone other than himself speaking for me.

"Really Mr. President, you'd rather come back with us, who would definitely manhandle you?" Lieutenant Kwan asked.

"We won't let her," father jumped in.

Lieutenant Kwan raised her finger to my father. "Your opinion doesn't count."

"Deal," I said.

"Don't do this. It will open the door to the extinction of humans as we are," the president said to me.

"I will not be responsible for the death of a human being who makes the world a better place," I said.

"But what happens after that? It's not about now, it's about the future," the president said.

"I have made my decision," I said.

One of the soldiers went into the car brought out a preservation sample case. She walked up to me and took out a needle. A needle wouldn't go into my body, except at a weak spot on the back of my neck, which is where she directed it. After she drew my blood, she attempted to cut locks of my hair, but their scissors kept breaking. I had to pull out three strands and give them to her.

After they got their samples and let father go, the whirling of helicopter got louder. I asked, "One of yours?"

Lieutenant Kwan got into her vehicle with the other soldiers. "Nope and, from the looks of that chopper, it's not coming to rescue anyone."

"Why would you say that?" father asked her.

"Who sends one helicopter to rescue the President of the United States?" Lieutenant Kwan said. She drove away, only to stop a mile later and have one of her soldiers shoot out one of the tires on our car. Then, they continued driving away.

The president and father were looking up at the helicopter, so they didn't see the soldier shoot out our tire and leave us stranded in the desert. Father asked, "Who is it?"

"Adam," I said, trying my best to mask the pain from my earlier injury.

Father's face was flushed and the president looked at him understanding the emotion. "I take it that Adam is bad news?" he asked. I nodded my head. "Do we have any weapons?" he asked.

"There is a pistol in the glove compartment," I said. The president walked to the car and retrieved the gun. Then, he saw the cell phone on the seat of the car, ducked lower and made a call, hoping I hadn't seen him. He returned to his position next to us and watched the helicopter.

Looking up, I said, "Did you get reception?"

The president smiled and said, "Yep."

"How long do we have before the entourage comes?"

"Ten or 15 minutes," he said with a frown.

"We should get in the car and run for it," father said.

"They shot out one of the tires," I said, "Unless one of you can change a tire in seconds, we are sitting ducks."

From the sky, a mass fell from the helicopter. It made a deep indentation in the ground when it hit. Dust rose around the mass and, when it settled, we saw Adam. He landed on his right knee and left foot and wore his usual black, hooded sweatshirt, a plain grey t-shirt and jeans.

Kyle

8:20 AM

The agents had taken over the room. They were searching it as if they owned the place. I walked over to the head agent and asked him, "What's your name, sir?"

"Benedict," he said, checking my father's laptop and not looking at me.

"Father made a deal with the White House. He was promised to be freed if he handed back the president."

He looked at me as though I was a naïve child and laughed, "Sure, we will let the man who is responsible for kidnapping the President of the United States waltz away from here because he had a change of heart." He brushed by me to the bathroom door and banged on it. "General, you have a minute left."

"That's all I need," father said.

Just then, the door was kicked open. A woman with dreadlocks, wearing a black pantsuit and white shirt with a black handkerchief around her nose and mouth entered the room holding two 9mm handguns complete with silencers. As she walked in, she fired four shots, every one hitting a CIA agent in the middle of his head. A barrage of bullets were fired at her from the remaining agents. She tumbled to the ground, using her right leg to sweep the nearest agent to the floor. Then, she used his body as a shield as she lay on the floor. The agents fired at her not caring that their bullets were killing one of their own. I couldn't see her as she was tucked underneath the dead agent. When the agents stopped shooting, there was silence in the room; there was no way she could be alive. An agent walked toward the body and, abruptly, her hands tucked out from behind the armpits of the dead agent. She fired four more shots, each landing in the middle of an agent's head. With superhuman strength, she flung the dead body at the agent approaching her, causing him to hit the floor. She jumped to her feet, ducked three shots from two agents and broke the shooting arm of the agent closest to her. Then, she kicked the gun from the second agent's hand and fired bullets into both of their heads. The last agent, Benedict, was trying to reload his gun, while the agent on the floor was pushing the dead agent off of him. She had her guns pointed at the two of them and they were quick to raise their hands in surrender. She didn't waste a bullet or have a scratch on her. I was bewildered. She had walked into a room filled with 12 armed men and killed 10 of them, while taking two prisoners, all in less than three minutes. It took me a while before I realized that I was in the room and not watching a movie. When I made this realization, I quickly raised up my hands in surrender.

"Room is secured," she said.

The man who walked into the bathroom was my father, the man who always gave his heart to me when we were alone. The man who walked out of the bathroom was General Coriolanus Cole, the man who demanded perfection from me in everything I did.

He looked at the two agents and said, "Kill them." She fired two bullets, not giving the agents a chance to plead for mercy. I looked at my father, confused. "Sloane, how many times have I told you to look the perfect soldier you are?"

"You have told me 2,345 times," she said, her voice soft and smooth. From her eyes, high cheekbones and skin complexion, I figured that she was Native American.

"And why haven't you gotten rid of the dreads?" my father asked.

"You haven't ordered me to change them," she said with a smirk.

Father sighed. The odd thing was that he made a concerted effort not to look me in the eye. "How is the outside parameter?"

"Six other CIA agents, KIA. Your other son is alive, although beaten unconscious," she said.

"Next time, don't leave him alive on my account," father said, walking past me, taking the signed papers and the briefcase.

"Aren't you going to look at me?" I said, almost in tears from the flippant manner in which he told Sloane to kill my brother. We were nothing to this man; he knew we would be coming and used us for his grand design. The man was a robot and he had treated us as machines from the day we were born. At least my brother was smart enough to have figured it out, while I the fool; I believed that a man of his caliber just never showed his love for his family.

"We are out of here," he said to Sloane, heading out the door.

"How long have we been your pawns!?" I screamed at him.

He ignored me and walked out the door. Sloane put her guns into their holsters, looked at me and whispered, "Don't believe the hype. He ordered me to watch over you, your brother and your mother for years."

"Sloane!" my father screamed out from the hallway.

She gave me a quick salute and ran out the door.

Adam

I stood up in the middle of the isolated desert. The last time I felt this type of heat was in Yemen. In front of me was the president, Professor Kozlov and Eve. This wasn't in the plan. Eve was stronger than I was and, if she was protecting the president, then this was a failed mission before it started. However, something was different about her. Her eyes were heavy, she could barely stand and I could smell her wounds. She was dying.

"Professor Kozlov, how has your day been?" I asked.

"Mind blowing," he said. I smiled.

I looked at the president and he looked at me. We didn't have any words to share. Then, I said, "Eve." I felt like Odysseus seeing his wife after decades lost at sea.

"Adam," she said trying to be strong, but even her frailty came out in her words. "You did say you would kill me when we met next," she said, attempting, but I could tell that she was preserving her strength.

"Hopefully, not today," I said. "You may go," I said it like I was the emperor of their lives, which, in a way, I kind of was. As all three began walking past me, I said, "The two of you can go, but not him," I said as I pointed at the president.

"Great," she said. "Shame on me for thinking this was going to be easy." She stood in front of the two men.

"Eve, you are dying. If you don't enter the cocoon state soon, you will die," I said. Then, I looked at the professor and said, "Save your daughter."

"Eve! It's a fruitless fight. You've done more than enough for him," the professor said.

The president stepped in front of her and put his hand on her shoulder. "Your work is done, Eve. I am more grateful than you can ever imagine, but it's time for the adults to take care of themselves."

"Listen to him," I said. "He is the ruler of the free world."

"You want to kill him," she said.

I forgot that she could read my mind. Then, I said, dragging out the word, "Yes…"

"Why?" she asked already knowing the answer.

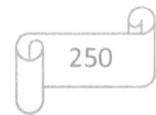

In that moment, she gave up her plans in her thoughts, "You are stalling for backup," I said.

Just then, she jumped into the air, rotated twice like a ball and landed hard on the ground, face and hand first, digging into the Earth with lightning speed, her legs acted like hands in which she clutched both the professor and president. She dragged them into the Earth as she dug deeper and further away like a badger. All of this happened in three seconds. I stood there awed by the magnificence of her actions. I had never done that before and, frankly, I wasn't even aware that I could do what she just did, but, then, first things first.

She had basically made a tunnel in the Earth and I quickly chased after them. It took me no time to catch up to them as she was using the last of her strength to dig the tunnel. She detected me approaching and dug back up to surface. Then, she flung the professor and president out of the ground and bounced out of the hole to her feet. As I raised my face up out of the hole, she punched me so hard that I flew out of the hole and 20 yards across the desert. Before I could take a second to breathe, she was on me, lashing me with punches. With each punch, she got weaker as did the punches, giving me time to recover. I kicked her sharply in the jaw, throwing her violently onto her back.

We both stood and stared at each other. She knew it was a lost battle, yet she was still ready to die fighting. "Let me have him, Eve. We can fight another day."

"Never!" she said and rushed me, throwing punches. I dodged every one of them. She had lost her speed and I just shoved her off.

This gesture peeved her and she dove at me. I grabbed her by the arm and flung her hard onto the ground, my two hands pressing on her neck. "Let me do what I came to do."

"Never!" she said, dying.

"What is wrong with you?" I asked with my hands still around her neck.

Then, I heard the click of a gun. I ducked and the bullet flew past me. On the other end of the gun was the president. He kept firing until his gun was empty. With the speed of a cheetah, I moved left to right, dodging all the bullets. When he ran out of bullets, my eyes were red with anger. The quills had risen all over my body, tearing through my clothing. I fired ten quills from my body at him. They hit him in various spots on his body and he fell to the ground. As he fell, he hit the back of his head and went unconscious. I was going to tear his head from his body. Just then, Eve grabbed my leg.

"Let him live and we will make a symphony together," she said.

Just the sight of her dying was too much to bear. She was flesh of my flesh, the bone of my bone. We were the only two in this cursed world and I was responsible for her death. I could hear the choppers coming from miles away. I had less than a minute to kill the president.

"Just do what you want to do with him," the professor said as he fell to his knees, pointing at the president, "but, please, please don't kill her."

"What have I done?" I asked myself. In that split second, I grabbed Eve and, carrying her in my arms with the greatest love I was capable of giving, made 20 giant leaps across the desert. When I landed, I ran into the desert and, with all my might, all my strength, all my love, ran until I was positive that no one would ever find us.

About the Book

The *Symphony of Extinction* was one of the first books I wrote that rebelled against every part of my original thought. With all of my books, I try to let them carve out their own paths, while still maintaining control in regard to where I want the story to go. However, the *Symphony of Extinction* did not respect that path. I found the characters unpredictable and often wrote wondering what would happen next. During the writing process, I experienced a period of writer's block. As I pondered what to do, I read William Shakespeare's *Coriolanus*. Once I digested the magnificence of Shakespeare's words, I was able to write again; however, the book that I finished was not the book that I had started writing.

I have always been a big fan of Storm from the X-Men. I've long had a desire to write a book about her, but I wasn't patient enough to wait to get the necessary rights from Marvel. Instead, I decided to write my own black female superhero and Eve was born. While I wanted to create a superhero, I wanted to do it right and rationally answer all of the impossible questions.

The best part of the book to me was that while Eve was engaging as a character, all of the other characters in the book were just as engaging.